The
RICH
Young Ruler

Sally —
I hope this book helps you
on your journey to becoming a
Rich Young Ruler —

2-7-19

Dan Newberry

ISBN 978-1-64299-927-3 (paperback)
ISBN 978-1-64299-929-7 (hardcover)
ISBN 978-1-64299-928-0 (digital)

Christian Faith Publishing, Inc.
832 Park Avenue
Meadville, PA 16335
www.christianfaithpublishing.com

Printed in the United States of America

My friend Senator Dan Newberry is an extraordinary man of God. In his new book, *The Rich Young Ruler*, he tells the story of two brothers who were courageous enough to believe what God says about them and pursue God's best. This story will change the way you view your future and inspire you to live and dream big.

—John Bevere, author/minister,
Messenger International

In a modest and readable style, Newberry gets straight to the point; the point being true success in life. This book is for everyone who ever thought, "I want to be better and I want do better." These are the heartfelt insights of a business and political leader who believes and lives what he writes.

—Mark Rutland, president of Global Servants,
and former president of Oral Roberts University

Dan's book, *The Rich Young Ruler*, is relevant to anyone facing adversity in their everyday life. This book challenges our definition of "success" and celebrates those who have overcome many trials and have held true to their beliefs in pursuit of their goals.

—Pastor Paul Daugherty,
Victory Church

In our lives, the pursuit of knowledge takes many forms. There is the obvious structured learning environment of school, but perhaps the biggest lessons in life are learned outside the classroom as we open ourselves up to the wealth of knowledge present in the people who come in and out of our lives. Such is the message of Dan's book, *The Rich Young Ruler*.

—Dick Einsweiler,
Cornerstone Credit Union League Retired

The Rich Young Ruler addresses the importance of overcoming adversity and becoming fit financially. The keys to winning in life are being fit physically, mentally, emotionally, relationally, and in your finances. This is a must read for anyone wanting to win in their finances and in life!

—Coach JC, founder of CoachJC.com
and FitFirstResponders.org

Dear Reader, this book is the very essence of life and instruction in righteous that God would have all mankind experience and live out to His glory. This book explores the principle of how you can live a successful life, a life that will help you obtain even your most distant dreams and succeed in your most ambitious endeavors. The principle is easily understood, revealing how simple changes in your lifestyle will bring both the wisdom and integrity that will set the wheels of divine favor into motion, generating your success.

Read with an open heart to hear what the Holy Spirit is saying to you, and then put what you hear into practice, being a doer of the word and not just a hearer only.

—Revs. Robert and Reba Johnson

FOREWORD

I have known Dan Newberry on both a personal and professional level for many years. Dan will be the first to tell you that his life journey has not been perfect. He has had successes and he has had failures; he has experienced highs in life and he has experienced lows. What has made a difference is that through all Dan's experiences, he never stopped learning. The man understands the value of knowledge.

In our lives, the pursuit of knowledge takes many forms. There is the obvious structured learning environment of school, but perhaps the biggest lessons in life are learned outside the classroom as we open ourselves up to the wealth of knowledge present in the people who come in and out of our lives. Such is the message of Dan's book, *The Rich Young Ruler*.

In *The Rich Young Ruler*, we meet John and Chuck Kindig, brothers who feel trapped by fate. For generations, Kindig men have come of age and spent the rest of their years scratching out meager livings working as farmhands. John and Chuck's father often spoke to his boys about the importance of pursuing knowledge, but poor farmhands like the Kindigs had neither the time nor the resources to pursue formal education.

Thankfully, younger brother Chuck refused to allow life's obstacles to deter him from heeding his father's counsel.

Chuck was a consummate dreamer; today we might call him an "outside the box" thinker. He reasoned that knowledge could be pursued through many avenues, so he persuaded John to join him in approaching the one rich person they knew—Mr. Sellers, who owned the large farm where the brothers worked—to ask him to share the secret to his success. That one courageous act would reap benefits beyond the boys' wildest expectations.

Mr. Sellers had seen countless men come to work on his farm, only to squander their hard-earned wages through foolishness as they led lives without purpose or direction. But he saw something different in the Kindig boys, and that left him open to the idea of building into their lives. When he looked at John and Chuck, he saw two young men with enough humility to render them teachable. Sellers not only agreed to share from his life's experience but he also helped John and Chuck cross paths with others who had knowledge to share.

My own life is proof that when we choose to humble ourselves to seek knowledge from whatever sources it can be found and truly desire the understanding to wisely apply the knowledge we attain, then our lives will change. In the words of Mr. Sellers, "Quality of life, extent of knowledge and understanding, and ultimately, wealth, are determined by the choices you make. Choose well and you will have a good life. Choose poorly and you won't . . . The routine you establish for yourself builds discipline. As you live a life of discipline, you establish character. Good character is evidenced by integrity, and integrity will bring you into your destiny."

I won't tell you how the stories of John and Chuck end. You'll have to keep reading to see for yourself. Just know that, like all of us, they had to determine their own paths to pursue their dreams. I wouldn't be surprised if some of the twists and turns of John and Chuck's stories remind you of your own life's journey. Turn the page and start your quest for knowledge in the story of *The Rich Young Ruler*. I think you'll find it an interesting and very engaging read.

Dick Ensweiler
June 2017
Dallas, Texas

CHAPTER 1

That night, the evening sunset was breathtaking. The sky was a canvas awash in variations of pink and gold. It was almost too beautiful to be real. As the sun bid farewell, sinking just below the horizon, the searing heat seemed to relent, though the thick humidity did not. These are the kinds of sunsets people love, but Chuck and John, exhausted as they were from the day's labors, sat on the porch of the bunkhouse, unable to truly enjoy the sight.

It's not that the brothers didn't appreciate a good sunset; it's just that the work wore them almost senseless. But they weren't about to complain about their jobs. With so many of their friends on the unemployment line, they were lucky to have work that could pay the bills. The fact that the boys were young, single, and able to work long hours with no demands from a family, made them attractive workers in a crowded job market. It also made them tired. And after all that work, the meager wages they earned by the sweat of their brows provided just enough to get them by with a little money left over to send home to their mother—something they'd felt was their responsibility ever since the passing of their father a few years ago.

Hard labor was the only work they'd ever known. For generations, men in the Kindig family had worked the fields. It never even crossed a young Kindig man's mind to think of doing anything else. Kindigs came of age, went to work, and fully expected to die in the same fields they tended. It was their lot in life, and they just accepted it. Which is why John nearly choked on his coffee when Chuck spoke up that night.

"Why do you think Mr. Sellers is so wealthy?"

"I don't know—and frankly I don't care," replied John. "I'm just happy to have a job, and you should be too."

"You know I'm happy to have a job. I'm just asking a question. How is it that Mr. Sellers is able to hire so many men and still has money left to buy additional fields? Where does all that money come from?"

"You know he came from privilege," John said. "Dad always told us that the Sellers had everything, and if we ever got the chance to work for them, we should. Maybe if Dad had followed his own advice, he wouldn't have died working in Mr. Lackey's fields."

"I mean no disrespect to Mr. Sellers. He's a good employer. He's always been fair to us. He gives us a good place to live and decent pay. I know Dad would be happy that we're working for Mr. Sellers, but don't you think he ever wanted more for us? Don't you think Dad wished we would one day move beyond breaking our backs to make ends meet? I know one day you want to have a family of your own. Don't you want more for your son than for him to work ten or twelve hours a day and then collapse into bed, exhausted every night? There has to be more to life than this. If I've learned anything from watching Mr. Sellers, it's that having wealth is about more than social status. It's about options."

John just stared at Chuck. Those thoughts had to have been percolating in his mind for a long time. He couldn't remember when he'd ever heard his brother string together so many words. The words struck a chord in John's heart.

He looked out over the fields that had become so familiar. He knew the smell of the soil, the slope of the ground, the way the morning fog would settle in as spring and fall approached. With a quiver in his voice, John replied, "I know Dad always wanted more for our family than his meager wages were able to provide. He told me once that he was sorry for the way we had to live. I could see the shame and regret in his eyes. I'll never forget that look. Dad wished he could have given you and me a chance at an education so we could get out of the fields. But then he was gone." John took a deep breath, wiped away the tear that had escaped and run down his cheek, and continued. "What choice do we have now? Dad is gone. We have a responsibility to Mom. We can't just run away to the university, as if we could ever afford it anyway. No, Chuck, our future is in the fields. Maybe our children will have it better someday, but we have responsibilities to attend to."

Chuck noticed, for the first time, all the wrinkles on his brother's face. John had the wrinkles of a man twice his age. Such is the toll hard labor in the hot sun exacts over the years. Chuck admired his brother's ability to work more hours than any other man in the field. John was the standard Chuck strove to reach. And now Chuck had to admit that his brother was right, the die had been cast. They were laborers, plain and simple.

Their mother's health was failing. She had not been the same since the passing of her husband, which had occurred three years earlier from a heart attack. While sudden, the event had not surprised anyone. Most men who worked the fields died before they reached the age of retirement. John, being a son and the oldest child, was now the patriarch of the family. His responsibilities left no time for foolish dreams of a different kind of life. His reality would be the same as his father's and his grandfather's before him.

But deep down in places John had forgotten existed, he desperately wanted to believe there was something more to life than their current circumstance. He just couldn't bring himself to give voice to that belief. What would be the good in that? More than once, his father had told him to never give up hope . . . but then he died in the fields. John was determined to accept what he had, be thankful, and try to make the most of it. But Chuck's words were stirring the embers of a fire John thought had long ago died out.

Suddenly, a smile broke across Chuck's face. "John, do you suppose there is a way for us to get an education?"

John, a little annoyed by the question, replied, "You know Dad wanted to send us to school. But money was, is, and will continue to be the problem. Tuition isn't free, you know."

"Listen to me, John, there's more than one way to get an education. Think about it. You are one of the finest farmhands around. How did you get to be so smart? Dad taught you everything he knew. Right?

"So why couldn't we apply the same tactic to finding out how to make money? Mr. Sellers is the richest man we know. Why don't we ask him how he became so rich? He knows something we don't, and if he is willing to share what he knows, we will have more knowledge than we do now. And that, my brother, is exactly what an education is—learning more than you know right now."

John considered his brother's idea. This was a new concept—pursuing an education *outside* of the university. What did they have to lose? Well, except their jobs, depending on how Mr. Sellers responded to their question.

After letting the idea roll around in his mind for a bit, John replied, "Even if Mr. Sellers did share some of his knowledge with us, it does us no good if we can't put it into practice. Right now, we spend every waking moment working to make enough to get by. We don't have any spare time to chase after ideas. It's a lost cause. We'd just agonize over what we can't do. Really, Chuck, some things are better left alone."

Not to be deterred, Chuck took a drink of his coffee, smiled, and said, "That doesn't sound like the John Kindig who once won a bet by single-handedly plowing more rows than any other hand on the farm, using the worst mule in the pack, to boot. That John Kindig didn't know the meaning of 'impossible.' But if you aren't interested in hearing what Mr. Sellers has to say, that's fine. I understand."

John sighed. It was obvious his little brother wasn't going to take no for an answer. So many times through the years, Chuck's big ideas and sly smile had enticed John into adventures. Early in their childhoods, John adopted the position that he should go along with Chuck's notions if for no other reason than to protect Chuck from himself. Once, while John was complaining about Chuck's antics, their father had told him, "John, blood is thicker than water. You take care of your brother. Family is the most important thing." That piece of advice had served as the guiding force in John's life. Everything he did was for his family, which was exactly what John was thinking of as he said his next words: "Okay, we will talk to Mr. Sellers. Whatever knowledge he shares, we will try to implement, as long as it does not keep us from taking care of our responsibilities.

It has to be agreed that if our work or Mom suffers, we will stop and tend to our business."

Chuck quickly replied, "Okay, it's a deal . . . although I don't know what could possibly go wrong. You know I always think things through before I jump in with both feet."

Both men laughed. "Think" and "Chuck" were rarely used in the same sentence.

"Good point, Chuck. We'd better go to bed, we've got a big day ahead of us tomorrow. You'd better ask that God grant you favor to talk with Mr. Sellers." The words sounded like a brotherly tease, but deep down, John knew that it would take a miracle for Mr. Sellers to agree to hear them—much less take their request seriously. As he lay down in his bunk, John said a prayer asking God to grant them favor with Mr. Sellers . . . and for the courage to change the course of their family for the better.

*****

The next morning, Chuck and John set out for the fields. Even when it wasn't time to plant or harvest, there was still plenty of work to be done on the farm. The weather had been finicky, even by Oklahoma standards, and Mr. Sellers was afraid the wheat crop might be suffering. It was all hands on deck, going through the fields to assess the condition of the crop. Add to that a fence in desperate need of mending and the daily chores of tending to the farm animals, and there wasn't much time left in the day for leisure.

John looked at Chuck and said, "We had better put the plan on hold till tomorrow. We can't afford to lose any time asking questions today. You know how the foreman gets when he thinks people aren't giving everything for the cause." Chuck agreed but secretly hoped for an opportunity to visit with Mr. Sellers right away.

At lunchtime the men sat down, tired and hungry. Chuck said, "I really hate doing this type of work. It's the same thing all day, every day, and no matter how much you do, it's never enough."

"I know what you mean," said John. "Did you notice Mr. Sellers out in the field with us today? He looked really intent. I think the foreman may be in trouble. They didn't appear to be on friendly terms, if you know what I mean."

"Did you talk to Mr. Sellers when you saw him?"

"No, it didn't seem like a good time."

Just then, Mr. Sellers walked up to the men. "Chuck, John, are you enjoying your lunch?"

John wasn't sure how to respond. He had seen Mr. Sellers ask men that question and then fire them on the spot for not working hard enough. Mr. Sellers did not look happy. His face showed the wear of years. Sellers's eyes bored holes through John as he stood there with an unreadable expression.

Chuck had witnessed the firing of a man the week before. While he hoped Mr. Sellers was just making chitchat, he knew that wasn't Sellers's style. Some of the workers had been complaining recently about the number of hours they were being worked and the pay they received. All that complaining tended to snowball, decreasing productivity as the grumbling increased. But he and John had worked harder than any man out there. Surely Mr. Sellers had observed their effort.

Finally, with a smile, Chuck replied, "Yes, sir. I have not had a better sandwich today."

John shot Chuck a look that would have made a dead man cower and said, "I believe my brother means that we are extremely grateful to have these sandwiches and look forward to getting back to work."

Mr. Sellers smiled. "You boys aren't in trouble, John. I'm glad to hear they're serving good food while you're working to see this harvest through to the finish. Keep up the good work. It'll be time to take the sickle to this wheat soon."

As Mr. Sellers turned and began to walk away, John could sense his brother's anxiety over missing the opportunity to strike up a conversation with the man. He told Chuck, "Now isn't the time. Just let him go."

Mr. Sellers stopped in his tracks and turned around. He may have been up in years, but his hearing was impeccable. Perhaps this came from years of listening to men complain under their breath or from having to defend his business practices from those who wished to do him harm; whatever the case, he had honed his senses and never missed an opportunity to gain information. In a single motion, Sellers turned and stared straight at Chuck with the piercing gaze of a man not accustomed to being trifled with. "Do you have something you need to say, Chuck?"

Chuck, taken aback, didn't have time to pull his thoughts together. It was apparent that Mr. Sellers was expecting a complaint; his blue eyes intensely pierced through Chuck, daring him to say what was on his mind, and Chuck knew he had better not lie. "Well . . . yes, sir," Chuck started slowly. "John and I were . . . well, hoping we might . . . I mean, we wanted to know . . . ."

"Spit it out, son, I haven't got all day!" Mr. Sellers interrupted.

Chuck blurted out, "We wanted to know if you would teach us how to become wealthy." He knew as soon as the words came out of his mouth that he had said the wrong thing. A look of bewilderment showed on Sellers's face. Chuck began to prepare himself for the scolding he knew his brother would deliver as soon as they returned to the bunkhouse for the night.

John added slowly, "Mr. Sellers, you know we come from a poor family. I believe my brother meant to ask if you would mind sharing some of the knowledge you have obtained while becoming wealthy. We were thinking such knowledge might help us change our family's future for the better."

Sellers knew the Kindig family well. He had tried for years to persuade the elder Kindig to work for him, but could never convince him to leave Mr. Lackey. Lackey never respected Kindig's loyalty. After the man's death, Lackey only assisted with funeral expenses because other workers threatened to walk off the job if he didn't.

After a moment of consideration, Mr. Sellers finally spoke. "Boys, we have a lot of work to do today. Come see me tonight in my office after the work is finished and we can talk. See you tonight."

Chuck and John watched as he walked away. Learning from the earlier mistake, neither said anything until they knew Sellers was out of earshot. John slowly removed his hat and hit Chuck with it. "What were you thinking? He could have fired us for asking such a question on the busiest day of the year!"

Chuck replied, "Well, it worked didn't it?"

The foreman called the men back to work. Lunch was over. A long, hard afternoon of work remained to be done. The afternoon would fly by as the brothers' thoughts were consumed with possibilities of what that evening's meeting with Mr. Sellers might hold.

CHAPTER 2

John and Chuck arrived at Mr. Sellers's office just as the sun started its descent behind the horizon. Neither had been to the boss's office before. As a matter of fact, other than the foreman, none of the workers went to the "big" office unless they were being fired. John's quiet knock at the door was answered with permission to enter.

To the brothers' surprise, the office was plain and sparsely furnished. Whitewashed walls were mostly bare, save for one picture of Mr. Sellers's parents that hung alone above the small woodstove. In front of a nondescript desk covered with orderly stacks of papers sat two straight-backed wooden chairs. Along the far wall was a cot, much like the ones the boys slept on in the bunkhouse. The most noteworthy feature of the space was a large window that looked down onto the fields. Mr. Sellers was sitting behind his desk reviewing some papers while glancing periodically out the window at the men still putting up the last of the equipment. The light coming from the oil lamp on the desk shone on Mr. Sellers's face, illuminating deep creases in his brow. He was obviously deep in thought.

John and Chuck stood in the doorway, not sure whether they should take a seat or stay standing. Sellers looked up after a few minutes and said, "I'm sorry, boys. Please come in and have a seat."

John and Chuck had just taken their seats when the foreman came in. "Mr. Sellers, you wanted to see me," the foreman said with a hint of annoyance that seemed to indicate he was less than thrilled to have been summoned to the office at the late hour.

"Clark, I want you to review the harvest estimates before you call it a day. It seems we are several bushels off from the anticipated yield. Let's make sure we're not overlooking anything."

For what seemed like an eternity, Clark just stared at Mr. Sellers. Finally he replied, "Sir, the men are exhausted. I'm exhausted. We have all put in a hard day's work. I am certain the figures are correct based on what I saw today, but, if you'd like, perhaps a review could be done in the morning?"

"Clark, I understand you're tired, having been up for two days straight dealing with new calves and cleanup from these late spring storms. However, I will have the information tonight. I will give you a choice—either you can get it for me or I will, but if I have to do it, perhaps that's a sign that it's time you find another place to work." Mr. Sellers's voice remained even as he spoke to Clark. His expression never changed. When a man was challenged out in the fields, emotions surged and voices rose as sharp words were exchanged. John and Chuck were amazed at the way Mr. Sellers remained so in control of his emotions.

Clark hung his head, knowing he'd crossed a line, and he quietly responded, "Yes, sir, I will get it done. Anything else?"

"Nothing for now. Once the harvest is in, we will give the workers some time off. Now get to it."

As Clark turned to leave, he noticed Chuck and John for the first time. An inquisitive look crossed his face, but he said nothing. As he walked from the office, the boys heard him yell, "Let's wrap this up for the day. All hands on deck!" Everyone in the room knew Clark had shouted loud enough for the brothers' ears to hear.

Mr. Sellers looked at the boys and said, "Normally I would expect you to help Clark take another look around, but you've done your part and I'm curious about your question from earlier today. You asked me how to become wealthy. Why would you ask such a question?"

Chuck and John looked at each other, trying to decide who should speak first. They had come straight from the fields and had not discussed who would take the lead. Thankfully, the noise coming from outside distracted Sellers and gave the boys a moment to think about how to proceed. Clark was hollering at each farmhand, asking them to report on the areas they had inspected that day. Numbers and details were being shouted back and forth and Sellers's face indicated he was consumed with mental calculations as the men shouted back their reports.

John spoke up, "Sir, you know our family has never had much. You knew our father. You know he died working in the fields, trying to provide for his family. We are thankful to have jobs. However, we are hoping to learn how to become wealthy so our future children can have hopes for a better future with fewer hardships and more opportunity."

Chuck added, "We know if we don't change what we do, all we can expect is the same life our father had and his father had before him. The problem is, we really don't have the foggiest idea where to start to change the course of our lives. Since you are the most successful man we know, we thought we'd start by asking you."

Just then Mr. Sellers said, "I understand, boys. Wait just a minute. Clark! Get in here."

Clark appeared almost immediately. "Yes, sir?"

"Clark, I just heard the numbers being shouted and I am certain the mistake is in that last area. Check with that man. Either we've had half a field wiped out by these spring storms, or he didn't give a full count for his area."

"Yes, sir," said Clark.

Mr. Sellers looked at the boys. It was obvious he was still paying close attention to the counts being performed outside, even as he considered the boys' words. Slowly, he began his response. "Chuck . . . John . . . you want to change your status in life. Do you believe wealth is the answer?"

John looked intently at Mr. Sellers and then cautiously said, "I'm not sure I understand your question."

Mr. Sellers got up and walked over to the window that looked out over the vast farmland. Growing up on this farm had been a great blessing. He remembered years spent working beside his father, learning the trade and becoming the benefactor of his father's wisdom. He'd never found the right woman with whom to settle down and raise a family. Since he had no wife, no children of his own, he'd poured himself into the farm; every effort had been given to its expansion and proper care. Now these young men sat before him, seeking his counsel. Sellers knew the best way to help John and Chuck would be to first give them a proper foundation. "John, do you think money will solve your problem? Do you think happiness rests in having money?"

John's first thought was that this was a trick question. He knew that if he said money was the key to happiness, he would appear shallow. But their family was broke and money would make a big difference in their quality of life. As John looked at his brother, the confusion on Chuck's face said he'd be no help answering the question. John started to reply "Well, sir, certainly you are aware of our family's status . . . ," but his words were cut short when Clark barged into the room, out of breath, giving John more time to compose his thoughts.

"You were right, sir! That man failed to count all of his rows, which threw the count off. We are now back on track with the annual estimate. You never cease to amaze me, sir," Clark said with a beaming smile.

"Good. Let's get everything buttoned up for the night and give tomorrow off to everyone who worked today. After basic daily chores, everyone can have a rest. Also, please close the door on your way out." Mr. Sellers said all of this without ever looking away from the window. "You were saying, John?"

John began again slowly, "Sir, you know our family history. While we are simple people, we still have needs. Money would certainly make a difference in our situation."

Mr. Sellers shot back quickly, "Well, if money is the issue, why don't you ask for a raise?"

Chuck kicked John's shin and looked at him with eyes narrowed. John knew why Chuck had reacted so quickly. The last few men who had asked for a raise were fired on the spot and they had not found work since.

John quietly responded, "Sir, we would never take advantage of your graciousness. We are thankful for the jobs we have. I hope I haven't offended you . . ."

"Please stop with the pleasantries, John. I have men here all day long buttering me up, looking for something. Just shoot straight with me. Are you really here to ask for a raise?"

John replied with empathy, "Sir, we do not want your money. Our question is sincere. We really are trying to glean from your knowledge, in hopes of changing our position in life. Dad used to tell us, 'No matter what you do, boys, get an education. In all your gathering, get knowledge.' However, we can't afford to go to the university. We are only coming to you to ask that you share your knowledge."

Mr. Sellers looked deep into the boys' eyes. They had the eyes of their father. He knew their father well and had attended church with him on many occasions. "You know that instruction your father gave you is from the Bible, don't you? It's found in the book of Proverbs. Your father was absolutely correct, knowledge is one key component to success, but there is a second component. Once you have the knowledge, you have to act on it, otherwise you are a fool. Attaining knowledge is only half the puzzle. Understanding how to apply that knowledge is the second half."

This was new information. Their father often spoke of pursuing knowledge, but never mentioned this second part called "understanding." The brothers sat silently thinking. Finally Chuck replied, "If understanding is the key to unlocking the power of knowledge, how do we gain understanding?"

Mr. Sellers watched as the men put the last of the equipment away in the barn and closed the doors. The smell of fresh soil mingled with the smell of impending rain—another storm was brewing. As the clouds were gathering on the horizon, Sellers watched Clark clap the men on the back, giving them praise for beating the storm, getting the harvest in, and completing the inspection and counts on time. As each man was paid for his work, a couple of the men headed directly to the company store. The store was a convenience for the workers, a place they could go to stock up on supplies without having to find a way to cover the distance into town. Unlike company stores on other large farms, Mr. Sellers did not mark up the cost of items to take advantage of his workers, nor did he offer items on credit. Some companies used the "store" to get their workers so far in debt that they could not leave. He'd always viewed such a practice as nothing more than a legal version of slavery.

"John, Chuck, do you see those men walking into the store?" Neither brother could see out the window, so they both stood and joined Mr. Sellers where he stood.

"Yes," they replied, almost in unison.

"Those men worked all week. They earned their pay. What do you suppose they will spend it on?"

John knew the men well. A few of them claimed to be family men, though no one had ever seen so much as a picture of their families. They blamed Sellers for not paying them enough to send for their families. In fact, John had overheard the men complaining just yesterday, saying their pay was not enough for the job they were asked to do. But these same men came to the fields day after day, hung over from consuming illegal hooch they'd purchased from a bootlegger the night before.

Chuck answered Mr. Sellers's question with a slight laugh under his breath, "I'll bet they are headed for the tobacco aisle."

"These men continually complain that they do not make enough money to send for their families. However, when paid, they make a beeline for tobacco or other such nonsense in the store. Or worse yet, they are first in line at the bootlegger to give him their hard-earned money. What does that tell you about their priorities? These men do not care about having their families close, they only care about their immediate need . . . or so their choices would indicate." Mr. Sellers now looked directly at the boys as he said, "Quality of life, extent of knowledge and understanding, and ultimately, wealth are determined by the choices you make. Choose well and you will have a good life. Choose poorly and you won't."

Both boys stood silently by Mr. Sellers, wondering if he was going to add anything else. After the comments had had time to sink in, Mr. Sellers spoke. "Do you understand what I am saying?"

"Yes, sir."

Out the window, John saw two men coming out of the bunkhouse gripping their coffee cups. John knew the cups were full, but you'd be hard-pressed to find a drip of coffee in them. Both men sat down on the steps of the bunkhouse and began drinking. John knew they would be there all night until the bottle they kept hidden under the loose floorboard was empty. "Mr. Sellers, I understand these men are wasting their money. However, neither Chuck nor I drink or smoke. How are we making poor choices?"

"John, understand this has little to do with the specifics of their situation. The problem is their outlook. They are only looking for immediate gratification and not thinking about the impact their choices have on their future. They don't think about how good it would feel if their children or wife were here with them. If they did, they would drink less and save more. They only think about how that cup will make them feel in about an hour. Imagine what different choices would be made if they thought about the long term. The outcomes of life are being shaped every day by choices made. Do you understand?"

Chuck replied, "Mr. Sellers, what you are saying is if we think about our choices, we will control the outcome. So, if we choose to spend . . ."

Mr. Sellers interrupted Chuck. "It's not just about spending. You make choices in every area of your life—money, time, companions, and much more. Make good choices and you will have good results. It's actually quite simple. The routine you establish for yourself builds discipline. As you live a life of discipline, you establish character. Good character is evidenced by integrity, and integrity will bring you into your destiny."

Before either brother could comment, Mr. Sellers said, "We will have to cut this meeting short. I have another meeting to get to. Consider what we talked about tonight as your first lesson." Looking intently into the eyes of each brother, he continued, "You understand this principle better than you think. It was exercised when you took the initiative to come see me tonight. Think about how you can apply what you've learned here. I'll expect a report tomorrow. Good night, men."

John and Chuck walked to the door, leaving Mr. Sellers staring out the window at the darkening sky. Chuck turned and said quietly, "Thank you, Mr. Sellers." The door closed behind them with a click.

CHAPTER 3

As Chuck and John walked back to the bunkhouse, they discussed what Sellers had said. The sun had long since set and now only the moon lit their path. The coming storm brought a change in the direction of the wind and a cool breeze was blowing. The boys fully understood the message Sellers was trying to get across but came to a roadblock when considering how to apply the knowledge he'd shared.

John, weary from the day's work and from rehashing the same points with his little brother, stopped in the middle of the road and said, "Chuck, we're not going to come up with all the answers tonight. I told you when we started that finding the time and energy to make changes would be the hardest part."

Chuck, feeling the same frustration, replied, "This should be simple. Sellers said that if we make good decisions, we will have good results. He said it's all about establishing a routine that will give us discipline, which will build our character, increase our integrity, and lead us into our destiny. I just don't know how to get started.

"You remember how Dad always said when we need direction, we should pray and let God show us the way? Before we knock off for the night, let's pray like Dad suggested and see what happens."

John kicked the dirt in frustration as he looked off into the distance. "Do you really think that will work? Dad was constantly asking God for a better life and was rewarded with a heart attack in the fields. I'm not certain God really cares about our life or the direction we take."

"John, we don't know that God didn't give Dad some direction. Maybe Dad didn't execute it because he didn't know how. Dad was a simple man, just like us. Perhaps working in the fields was Dad's desire. One thing I do know is that he never questioned whether God cared for him. I just think we ought to try the prayer thing. I mean, what can it hurt? It got us the meeting with Sellers."

John found it hard to refute Chuck's argument. He remembered all the great things their father had said about God as the boys were growing up. He remembered his father being thankful they had food on the table, even though at times it wasn't much. He remembered the many times he'd seen his father singing in the fields, eyes to the heavens like he was actually praising God in the midst of his backbreaking labor. He remembered seeing his father asleep with his Bible in his lap, knowing he had been reading God's Word and praying for his sons. Finally John said, "OK, Chuck, I guess it can't hurt anything. I'll join you in praying and asking God for direction."

The brothers entered the bunkhouse, and Clark stepped into their path. "Well, boys, did you enjoy a relaxing time tonight with Sellers? Because the rest of us were busting our backsides covering your chores while you yucked it up in the big office. Who do you think you are, anyway, having a private meeting with the boss? Don't you understand the pecking order? You report to me. If you need to ask a question or get a message to the boss, it goes through me. He's a busy man. He doesn't have time to deal with farmhands."

"Clark, you're way out of line," Chuck said, stepping into Clark's personal space. "We were invited to the office by Mr. Sellers himself. You're just sore because we saw you get put in your place by the old man. Not our fault that you . . ."

"Chuck, we're done here," John cut in. "Clark, we know you're our boss. You should know that our conversation tonight with Mr. Sellers had nothing to do with you or your place of authority. We had a few simple questions for him that had nothing to do with our jobs—or yours. It was a personal matter—and by personal, I mean it's none of your business. Now we're going to hit the sack. Goodnight."

The boys stepped around Clark and proceeded to their bunks. That night, they prayed for wisdom harder than they'd ever prayed before. Time would tell if their prayers were heard.

*****

It was just after eight when Mr. Sellers walked into the cafe to meet with Joseph Hillman. He hated to be late to any appointment, but he just couldn't bring himself to rush John and Chuck out of his office.

Joseph Hillman was a tall, slender man with hair as black as night that was always slicked back perfectly. His tan suit and crisp white shirt were pressed to perfection. Even at this late hour, his tie was still securely knotted at his neck. He sat at a table in the back corner of the cafe, legs crossed, holding a cup of coffee in one hand and a paper in the other. When he saw Mr. Sellers enter the cafe, he pushed the small, round glasses up on his nose and stood to greet the man.

Mr. Sellers approached the table. "Hillman, you checking the pricing on the crop I'll be bringing in soon?"

Joseph smiled as he shook Mr. Sellers's hand. "Perhaps I should. Wouldn't want to overpay. How are you, old man?"

"I'm pretty good. We've been working our fields with all the strange weather we've had lately. Doesn't look like we've fared too badly. Our wheat harvest should be a good one. It seems as though these last few years, the yield from my fields has been especially good. Day after tomorrow, we'll begin prepping the south fields. The north ones are ready for a break. But I know you didn't ask to meet at this time of night to hear about farming. What's on your mind?"

A look came across Joseph's face indicating something was wrong. "Well, I never can hide anything from you. I just wanted to let you know that I had some executive meetings over the past few days and it looks like the crop prices might not hold much longer. Our carryover stock is reaching capacity. The guys in charge are telling us we may want to let our farmers know there's change coming."

"That's why I like doing business with you. Where is the market headed?"

"I'm not sure. We're looking at the export needs currently. However, you might look to cotton. At least for the next two growing cycles. There's been an increase in demand and it doesn't look like our current suppliers are keeping up with it. Could be a great opportunity if you haven't already planted."

"Cotton . . . I know other farmers in the area have been planting that, but I never thought of trying it on my land. It's a temperamental crop to grow. Could you send the demand numbers to me? Could be a great project over the next few years."

"I guessed you would ask, so I brought them with me." Joseph reached into his bag and brought out some loose papers and a binder full of numbers.

Mr. Sellers looked around the diner at the other patrons. He hadn't yet made the leap to run electricity to his farm but certainly enjoyed the luxury of electric lights when in town. People were enjoying their meals and life was going on as usual. A mother and her son were eating at a table across the aisle, the boy talking nonstop and playing with his fork while his mother sat patiently trying to get him to eat his sandwich. Joseph spoke, bringing Mr. Sellers back from his thoughts, "Do you know them?"

"Sorry, Joseph. I was thinking about a conversation I had today with two of my employees. That little boy reminded me of how I've watched them grow up. They are good men, ignorant of the way the business world operates, but good-hearted. Their father worked for a farm down the way, however, so the boys never knew I was watching them grow up. Their father died in the fields a few years back. I hired them to work for me when Lackey wouldn't pay them a fair wage."

Joseph replied, "That must have been some conversation. I've never seen you so distracted when talking about business."

Mr. Sellers took a drink of his coffee, and after a long pause, said, "They asked me to teach them how to become wealthy. When I pressed them to tell me why they would ask such a question, they gave me a noble answer: 'To better the future of our families.' Their sincerity really took me aback. Most of the time these guys ask me for raises, only to squander the money on bootleg alcohol."

Joseph studied his friend's face. He could see that the conversation with the two young men had really affected him. "What did you tell them?"

"I gave them a lesson in what wealth isn't. I explained that wealth isn't just about getting more money. It's about the accumulation of wisdom and the employment of understanding to know what to do with that wisdom. I began to teach them how to think about decision-making processes. I hope they understood what I was trying to teach them. We'll see how they do with that lesson. I really need to figure out how to make them understand that life is about choices."

"Well, old man, I hope to meet these prodigies someday." Joseph paused and then added, "When you're done with your teaching, send them to me. If you think these boys hold enough promise that you're willing to take on a project like this, I will too."

Mr. Sellers looked across the table at his friend, shocked and amazed. He knew the kind of schedule Joseph kept and knew there was not a lot of room in it for silly pursuits. "You would do that? Why, I am in utter shock. That is incredibly kind of you."

"Listen, we only have a short time in life. If we don't invest in people, what will be our legacy? Besides, you must see something in these boys if you are willing to teach them. I respect you so much, that is all I need to know."

The men continued their conversation about the cotton markets, management strategies, coming rains, and everything in between until it was closing time. The men paid for their coffee and walked out onto the street. The promised rain was beginning to fall and a cool breeze was blowing. "Sellers, don't forget to send those boys my way when you think they're ready. Have a great night."

"Thanks for all the insight, for the heads-up on the crop prices, and for your willingness to assist with John and Chuck. Looking forward to sending you a bumper cotton crop. See you soon."

CHAPTER 4

The next morning came early for Chuck and John. Though neither brother would admit it, they had not slept much through the night. The rain from the night before had cooled things off and the smell of wet soil filled the air. The brothers walked to the south field after finishing their daily chores with the break of day. The farm was quiet as most men were either sleeping in to put off their daily chores or were still passed out from the previous night's festivities.

The decision to walk down to the south field was a random one. Both boys wanted to get out of the bunkhouse and enjoy the cool morning air. They figured a walk to the south field was as good as a walk anywhere else. The south field had not been plowed in months; grass and weeds had taken over. The field sat in a low valley surrounded on three sides by sloping hills. A stream ran down one of the hills, meandering right through the middle of the field.

The boys had walked in silence, each lost in his own thoughts, until John spoke, "Well, any good ideas yet?"

Chuck, looking rather desperate, replied, "No, I haven't had any ideas and can't say I see any burning bushes out here pointing the way, either."

Both men chuckled. "I don't suppose we would," John said sarcastically.

The men turned their attention to a discussion of the land in front of them. Farming was in their blood. It had been the family business for as far back as they could remember. What to do with a piece of ground to make it fruitful—now that was a problem they knew how to solve. They were so deep in conversation that neither man noticed Mr. Sellers as he walked up behind them.

"Beautiful day, boys. You're up pretty early. Why aren't you sleeping in like the rest of the men?"

Chuck and John turned around, startled to hear another voice behind them. "Good morning, Mr. Sellers," they said in unison.

"We were just looking at the south fields and discussing ideas of how to prepare them for seeding," Chuck said. "Besides, we didn't have any other plans for today anyway, and we're not late risers."

"You know, boys, I'm glad you're here. This gives us another chance to talk. I've really been thinking about your question, and there are a few more things I'd like to share with you. One comes to mind right now. Always remember, a man who will not work will not eat. Many men are enjoying a day off, not thinking about what tomorrow might bring. There is potential in every day. The smart man—the wealthy and successful man—understands this and thinks about tomorrow, about how his actions today can maximize tomorrow's potential. While thinking and planning may not look like work, it certainly is. It's a different kind of work."

John and Chuck looked at each other, not really knowing how to respond. When they thought of work, they only thought of hard labor. They'd never considered that planning was just as much work as plowing. The brothers went back to surveying the field, considering this new perspective.

After a few moments John asked, "Mr. Sellers, can you tell me why we don't work all the fields at the same time? This field looks like it hasn't been touched in a long time."

Mr. Sellers smiled. It was a sight neither of the men had seen many times before. The smile broke the hard, leathery countenance of the successful farmer, and a look of mischievousness took its place. "That is an excellent question, John. Running a farm is mostly management of assets. I only have so many men and so much time. In life and in business, you should never overextend yourself. We could have worked this field last year, but to do so, we would have had to pull men from other fields. If we pulled men from other fields, we might not have reached the desired production of either field because our workforce would have been spread too thin. Just because you can do something, does not mean you should. It goes back to choices. I think it was a good choice to let the field rest while we focused our labor in the other fields.

"Besides," Mr. Sellers continued, "I've always had trouble with this field. The water that runs through that stream during the rainy season overwhelms the field and the crops we plant here. When planting this field, I've had to haul in soil and add nutrients because the topsoil washed away. This year, however, I made a decision to do something different in this field. I'm going with a crop I've never planted before—cotton—and boys, I want you to take charge of the project."

Chuck looked at John in amazement. Neither of the men knew how to respond. They'd never been in charge before. What was Mr. Sellers thinking, entrusting them with charge of a project, especially this project that represented a brand-new crop start for the farm?

Mr. Sellers must have known what the brothers were thinking as the smile remained on his lips. "I have learned that the buyers of our crops are looking to diversify in the coming years. You boys are the first farmhands in all my years to ask questions and show an interest in advancement without the hidden agenda of digging for additional pay. I've judged that you are sincerely searching for knowledge and therefore have decided to reward you by giving you this opportunity. Understand this will be a great deal of work. However, if you listen to my instruction and show yourselves worthy, when the crop comes in, I will send you to sell it."

The look on Chuck's and John's faces was one of absolute shock. This pleased Mr. Sellers, mostly because it confirmed that the men understood the magnitude of what he was offering. In farm work, management of a field was never entrusted to the laborers. This work was reserved for the owner and his most trusted assistant. If mistakes or misjudgments occurred, they could cost the entire crop. Owners did not entrust just anyone with the job of securing their profits. But there was one more bombshell left to share. "One other thing," Sellers continued. "When we sell this crop, I will split the profits with you."

John slowly turned toward Sellers. The look of shock had been replaced with one of concern. He searched for words to reply to the old farmer. This offer surpassed anything he ever could have expected. Certainly he and Chuck had spent years working on farms and had learned a great deal from their father, but to be considered for this opportunity was almost more than he could take. Finally, with his voice choked by emotion, John asked, "Why us? We haven't been trained in management work. Shouldn't Clark do this?"

Chuck, too, was overwhelmed by emotion. As he looked at this field Mr. Sellers was willing to entrust to him and his brother, a tear escaped and slid down his cheek. The means to all his father had ever wanted for him now literally lay at his feet. This opportunity could change everything. This could be the first step in creating a better future for his family.

As Chuck pondered the implications of this generous entrustment, Mr. Sellers replied to John's question. "John, I told you before that life is about choices. I am making a choice to give you this opportunity and I am fully prepared to accept the consequences. All I ask is that you don't squander the opportunity that has been put in front of you.

"Understand, if you can be trusted with the small things, if you are diligent in what has been placed before you, if you give a hundred and ten percent in everything you do, opportunities for promotion will come. You've always been hard workers for me. You don't slack in the field, even when you had opportunity to do so. You've been faithful farmhands, which is why I am giving you this opportunity.

"This new job will not be easy. It will require the same commitment to hard work. Others will be jealous of your opportunity and will wonder why they haven't been given control of this field. They will find reasons to discredit you and will likely try to sabotage your efforts. Clark, at my direction, will assist you. He is a good man with a good heart, but he may not be happy at your new opportunity. Undoubtedly, he will wonder why I have not entrusted this field to his care.

"Most importantly, under no circumstance whatsoever are you to tell anyone you'll share in the profits. When completed with excellence, others will have no choice but to respect your efforts. Some will be critical, but remember that they have cast their lot in life. You cannot control them or what they say about you. You can only control *your* words and *your* actions. Stay focused and see what happens."

CHAPTER 5

Working in tandem with Mr. Sellers, Chuck and John developed a plan to prepare and plant the south field. It didn't take long for word to get around the bunkhouse that two of their own had been tapped for bigger things. At first, some men outright refused to work for the boys. When the men realized there were only two choices—work the south field for John and Chuck or hit the unemployment line—they resolved to show up each day but spend nearly all of their time on break. If the men managed to get any work done, it was sloppy and done at an agonizingly slow pace.

Clark proved to be of little to no help. The foreman who once could drive a group of men to complete the most herculean of tasks, now made excuses to cover for the lack of productivity. It was clear to John and Chuck that no respect would be given them by their coworkers. They would have to earn it.

Through dogged persistence, John and Chuck managed to have their team change the flow of the stream to better irrigate the field. They prepared the soil, rooting out the grass and weeds and adding the proper nutrients the cotton would need to grow. The brothers remained focused on the task at hand, even though several workers continued to criticize their inexperience. Chuck and John were no longer considered a part of the group. They weren't asked to join the other men for coffee in the evenings, they weren't called on to participate in friendly games of checkers or horseshoes, and they weren't included in weekend outings. Not all of the men treated them so coldly, but enough of them did so as to make things uncomfortable around the bunkhouse.

Chuck and John could not remember a time in their lives when they'd prayed so much. They knew that cotton was a temperamental crop to grow. Their cotton plants would need nearly a hundred and sixty days of good temperatures and just the right amount of rain to fully produce.

The brothers watched the skies, anxious for rain; then when the rain came, they prayed it would stop before the field became too saturated. They monitored each and every plant, looking for pesky boll weevils. They directed the men to hoe the field continually, to thin the crops and to keep the weeds at bay. They were as proud as new fathers when the first plants emerged from the ground. Each stage of development was a milestone for the brothers. When the flowers developed, they swore they'd never seen a more beautiful sight. As the bolls sprouted, grew and then burst open, revealing the gorgeous, soft, downy cotton, they whooped and danced like madmen.

After several months, the time came to harvest the cotton. Clark assisted the boys in dividing up teams to pick and weigh the harvest. The cotton was harvested by hand and placed in cloth sacks. Once a sack was full, it was weighed and then dumped in the wagon to await transport to the cotton gin. Once the harvest was brought in and the final bag weighed, the boys went to see Mr. Sellers. They found him standing in his office with papers in his hand, looking out the big window at the fields, obviously deep in thought. He was unaware the boys had entered the room until Chuck spoke.

"Mr. Sellers, we've harvested the cotton and it's ready to go to be ginned." Startled from his thoughts, Mr. Sellers dropped his papers. Chuck continued, "Oh, I'm sorry. Didn't mean to startle you. Let me help you with those."

As Chuck picked up the papers, Mr. Sellers sank down into his chair and let out a sigh. The boys had never seen the man so disturbed. John asked, "Is everything OK?"

Mr. Sellers smiled slightly and said, "Well, boys . . . I told you we'd been encouraged to diversify our crop production. A dear friend and colleague informed me when we went to market the price for wheat crops was not going to hold much longer. He is the one who encouraged me to focus on cotton. I listened to his advice and put you to work in the south field. In the meantime, I've received final numbers from the sale of our wheat crops. As my friend warned, the prices have dropped out of the wheat markets. I hope you're bringing me good news, as it looks like our only saving grace may be your cotton crop."

John smiled and said, "Sir, with all the work we put into maximizing the irrigation situation in the south field, added to the especially good weather we've had over this past growing season, I am proud to tell you the crop yielded three times what we expected! Clark and the workers are packing the last of the cotton into the wagons now to send it to be ginned before going to market."

Mr. Sellers jumped out of his seat, slammed his fists on the desk and peered at John over the rims of his glasses. "Three TIMES?! How can it be?"

Chuck, rather startled by the outburst from his usually restrained boss, placed the papers on the desk and replied, "We did what you told us to do. We followed the plan and the crops yielded more than we expected. We know the numbers are correct. John and I have reviewed the numbers personally four times."

Just then, Clark entered the room. Without taking his gaze off Chuck and John, Mr. Sellers said, "Clark—is this correct? That little field yielded three times what we expected?"

"Yes, sir, it did. I could hardly believe it myself. John and Chuck worked that field and the workers assigned to it with precision. They prepared the field for maximum productivity, and with the irrigation plan they devised, they were able to keep the moisture level of the soil constant throughout the growing season. I have never seen anything like it. We expected a decent return, but what we've ended up with is beyond anything I've seen in all my years in the field . . . it's absolutely amazing."

"Great work, men!" Mr. Sellers boomed. "I am proud of you for following instruction and giving your full effort to the task at hand. You made full use of the opportunity that was presented to you. Now, being true to my word, I want to include you in the entire process of getting the cotton to market. I'll make the arrangements at the cotton gin. After we've had the cotton ginned, we'll find a buyer for the cotton lint and then we'll meet with Joseph Hillman to sell the cottonseed. Joseph Hillman is a man I want you two to meet. I think he has a lot he can teach you. But first, let's see about finding an appointment at a cotton gin."

As Chuck and John left the office, they were surprised to see Clark waiting outside for them. "Men, there's something I need to say to you. When I heard about the opportunity Sellers gave you, I can't say I was happy. In fact, I was downright angry over his decision. I felt like it was my turn, and if Sellers was going to trust anyone with his land, it should have been me. I admit, in my anger, I didn't always give you my best effort. That was wrong of me. I hope you'll accept my apology. I've never seen a harvest like what we brought in from that little field. I still can't get over it. But what may have impressed me the most was the way you never gave up, even when it must have seemed like every single man on this farm was against you. You've earned my respect, that's for sure. There are still plenty of guys nursing a grudge, especially after the incredible harvest you brought in, but I want you to know you won't have a problem with me anymore."

The brothers were dumbfounded. They shook Clark's extended hand and muttered a thank-you or two, then headed toward the bunkhouse. This was definitely a breakthrough, but would the rest of the men feel the same way? As they approached the porch, they got their answer. A small group of men were huddled together talking in hushed tones. When they saw John and Chuck approaching, the talking ceased. Obviously, these men did not share Clark's opinion of the boys or their good fortune.

CHAPTER 6

Chuck and John were working on an old plow when they got the message that they were needed up at the big office right away. Fully expecting to visit with Mr. Sellers, they were surprised when they were greeted by an attractive young woman who was going through some papers in one of the straight-backed chairs in front of the desk. "Gentlemen, my name is Reba Johnson, Mr. Sellers's assistant. I hope I didn't call you away from your work at an inconvenient time. Mr. Sellers asked me to give you details about the trip to the cotton gin that is coming up day after tomorrow. You and Mr. Sellers will be following the wagons to the gin. He wanted you to have a chance to see the local gin and have the opportunity to visit with Nehemiah Fisher, the man in charge of operations at that facility. I've made all the arrangements, and Mr. Fisher will be expecting you at nine a.m."

The boys were taken aback by this confident young woman. They'd never known a woman who worked outside her home. Their mother, though she was a strong woman, had spent her life caring for her husband and family. Now here was this attractive woman sitting in a man's office, going over paperwork and giving out instructions about matters of business.

The brothers acknowledged the instructions and left the office, heading back to their work. John still didn't know what to make of Mr. Sellers's assistant. "What did you think of Reba? Seems strange for a woman to be working in an office. I mean, Mom always spent her time cooking, cleaning, doing laundry, and that sort of thing. She always left business matters to Dad."

"I rather liked her. She has the most beautiful eyes I think I've ever seen."

"I didn't even notice that she had eyes. I couldn't get past the fact that a woman was talking about matters of business. She's the first woman I've ever known to do that."

"I agree, I've never met a woman like Miss Reba. But I'm certainly glad I have now. Meeting her was a very pleasant addition to my day, and I hope it won't be long before our paths cross again."

*****

The day for the trip to the cotton gin arrived. John and Chuck met Mr. Sellers by the large storage barn after helping to hitch the last of the horses to the wagons. "Good morning, men. You two will ride with me in my car for the trip to the gin. I think you'll enjoy seeing the operations, and I know you'll enjoy meeting Mr. Fisher. He's seen quite a bit in his years and has a lot of wisdom he can share. Let's load up."

John and Chuck tried not to let on that they were giddy to be riding in Mr. Sellers's car. While cars were more prevalent in town, very few farm folk owned their own vehicles. Not even the horribly bumpy roads could dampen their enthusiasm to be on this outing. They watched ahead as the wagons full of cotton made their way along the route to the gin. Seeing all those huge wagons loaded down reminded the brothers again of the generous bounty of their first crop.

They pulled into the lot in front of the building housing the cotton gin and got out of the vehicle. Mr. Sellers told the boys to follow him, and they proceeded into the building where they were greeted by a rather short man with a round, red face and not a single hair on his head. "Mr. Sellers, I've been waiting for you. I trust all your wagons made it here safely?"

Mr. Sellers removed his hat and replied, "Yes, Mr. Fisher, they did. It's a pleasure to see you again. Let me introduce you to John and Chuck. They are responsible for this wonderful harvest. As a thanks for their hard work, I'd like to afford them the opportunity to gain a better understanding of the work you do here at the gin. You'd mentioned that you'd visit with them, and now here we are."

"Excellent. Right this way, gentlemen. Let me get all the paperwork in order so we can start putting your cotton through the gin. Once the work is underway, we can visit outside where things will be a little quieter."

As Mr. Fisher went off to notify his workmen that it was time to start weighing and processing John and Chuck's cotton, the boys wandered back outside. Mr. Sellers followed and in just a few minutes, the cotton was leaving the wagons and heading in to be ginned. The cotton would be processed and baled. The cotton seed would be bagged up and loaded back in the wagons for transport to the local grain elevator.

Mr. Fisher emerged from the building and came over to where John, Chuck, and Mr. Sellers were standing by the car. "So, gentlemen, Mr. Sellers tells me you have an interest in expanding your knowledge base. I must say, that is an admirable pursuit. I certainly will share with you everything I know about running a cotton gin, but the story of my journey to become operator of this gin may be of more interest to you."

"Anything you'd be willing to share would be much appreciated, Mr. Fisher," Chuck said. "My brother and I come from a long line of hardworking farmhands. We're proud of the work ethic they've passed down to us, but we've just been wondering if we could expect more from life. We weren't afforded the opportunity to attend the university, but we've found that the university isn't the only place you can get an education. People like you who have found success can educate us just as well as any book could."

"That's a wise observation, Chuck. You see, I never attended the university. I just happened to find myself in the right place at the right time and I paid attention. I envy your family life. My father died when I was only seven. My mom tried her best to hold our family together, but one by one, we drifted away. My two older brothers left home within two years of Dad passing away, then it was just Mother and me. I knew I had to find a job, so at the age of ten, I was hired on as a stock boy for the local grocer.

"Mr. Brown ran a tight ship. He didn't tolerate sloppiness, worked his employees hard, and kept a close eye on his bottom line, but he was always fair. He gave me a decent wage and a place to sleep in the back of the store. Every day I would watch Mr. Brown run his store. I paid attention to how he interacted with his customers, and then I made sure I followed his example down to the smallest detail. I kept the store neat as a pin, including my sleeping area in the back. I made sure I was the best employee Mr. Brown could ever hope to have.

"One day, a new customer came into the store. Mr. Brown greeted him, and the two men began to talk. This man was opening up a cotton gin in our town. I was fascinated as the man talked about this amazing machine and how much work it could accomplish. Every time that man came into the store, I made sure I was dusting shelves near him or stocking produce, just so I could hear about the progress on building the gin. I so wanted to work at that place! One day, I finally mustered the courage to talk to Mr. Brown about the possibility of going to work at the new cotton gin. I was thirteen years old.

"I could not believe my good fortune. Mr. Brown agreed to recommend me to Mr. Knoll, the owner of the gin. Mr. Brown's recommendation must have carried a lot of weight, because Mr. Knoll took me on. From day one, I learned all I could about the ginning operation. Even though I was working with men much older and more experienced than me, I distinguished myself by working hard and never complaining. I was not only trying to make a reputation for myself but I also felt I owed it to Mr. Brown to do a good job to prove he was right by what he said about me.

"Mr. Knoll stayed here in Chickasha for four years running this gin until he decided it was time for him to move on and open his next gin. When it came time for him to pick a successor to take over the operation, I was stunned to be called into his office and offered the job. I had just turned seventeen years old at the time and couldn't believe he would entrust the operation to me. In fact, I said as much to him. He told me not to let anyone look down on me just because I might not have years on my side. He said that in the four years I'd worked for him, I'd been an example for all his men and I'd earned my position.

"Unfortunately, not all of the men I'd been working with were happy about my promotion. Some of those men turned downright ugly when they heard that the kid they'd been working alongside would now be their boss. A few of them went to Mr. Knoll and tried to get him to change his mind about my promotion, telling him lies about my performance. But Mr. Knoll was no absentee gin operator. He'd seen firsthand my work ethic and dismissed the lies that were told about me.

"When the men saw they weren't gaining any traction with Mr. Knoll, they then tried to turn the rest of the workers against me. They reasoned that a gin couldn't run without help, so if they drove the help away when I took over I'd fall flat on my face. As one man and then another resigned, I started to wonder if maybe I was in over my head, but I refused to give up that easily. I was determined to prove to Mr. Knoll that I was worthy of the confidence he had in me.

"Eventually the day came when I was fully in charge of the gin. Though we'd lost some of our workforce, I was confident that things would be fine, because, to my surprise, I'd managed to hold on to some of the most seasoned men. I would soon come to regret the fact that some of them were still around. The first week that I was in charge, one of our customers came in to tell me that he'd found another gin to process his cotton. Since the man didn't really know me, I chalked the loss of his business up to his being hesitant to entrust his crop to a young gin manager. But when one of our biggest customers came in the very next week to tell us that he, too, planned to take his cotton to a gin in Texas, I began to think that there might be more to this loss of business than just nerves over a change in management.

"I had some experience working with that second customer, so when he told me he was taking his business elsewhere, I felt comfortable asking him some questions to get to the bottom of why he'd made that choice. It took a good deal of questioning but he eventually told me that word around town was that I had a problem with honesty. He said that someone with working knowledge of the gin had told him they'd seen me falsifying weights on some of the orders so I could keep either lint or seed back for myself to sell on the side.

"I think you can imagine how angry that made me! I assured my customer that there was absolutely no truth in that rumor and invited him to send some of his men to supervise the processing of his cotton, if that would put his mind at ease. My openness and transparency saved his business, and he's still one of my most loyal customers today, but at the time, I knew I had a problem I had to root out. I would not allow someone spreading false rumors from my own gin to intimidate me into giving up my position so they could have it for themselves.

"I went to Mr. Brown, my very first boss, to talk things over with him. That was one of the smartest things I could have done. After all his years serving the customers at his grocery store, Mr. Brown knew how to deal with people—both happy people and disgruntled people. He was able to give me some good advice about how to manage my workers and how to deal with those men who were still out breathing lies about me. Mr. Knoll kept in touch too. That man knew about the character of the people who were attacking me and he gave me great advice about how to respond. He reminded me that the only things needed to be successful were determination to stay the course and a firm commitment to run the gin with integrity. I tell you, if I hadn't had those two men in my life, I would have been sunk for sure. But thanks to them, I'm still here running a gin that is more successful than ever."

"What an incredible story," said Chuck. "You were lucky to be in the right place at the right time, I guess."

"Maybe that played a part in my story, but I don't think that's the real reason I am where I am today."

"So what do you think the secret is to your success?"

"Well, I've always paid attention. No matter the position, I was always listening and studying what those in positions of authority over me were doing. I learned about hard work and customer service from Mr. Brown. I learned about good business practices and the life cycle of cotton from Mr. Knoll. What I learned, I put into practice faithfully. If you'll do a good job, people will notice. If you do a good job, people will be willing to entrust you with more responsibility and sometimes even stake their reputation on you, like what Mr. Brown did for me. Be attentive, determined and faithful.

"Above all else, guard your integrity. The only thing that saved my position was the fact that when put under scrutiny, my integrity was found to be above reproach. You see, a man is known by his word. Circumstances and situations can come your way in life that will take things from you, but nothing can take your integrity. To lose that, you have to give it away."

"Nehemiah, we've taken up enough of your time," said Mr. Sellers. "I certainly do appreciate you visiting with us today. I think you've given these young men a lot to think about. We'll let you get back to your operation, and we'll head back to the farm. Our men will bring the bales of cotton lint and the cottonseed back to the farm once you and your crew have finished the ginning."

CHAPTER 7

Chuck and John walked from the bunkhouse toward the main house and Mr. Sellers's automobile. Today they were scheduled to drive into town to meet Mr. Hillman and sell the cottonseed. The boys had never heard Mr. Sellers speak of a man the way he spoke of Mr. Hillman, so they were excited to meet him in person to see what all the hype was about. Mr. Sellers was standing on his front porch waiting on the boys and he greeted them warmly, "Good morning, boys. It's a great day, isn't it? Today, you'll get the chance to see the grain elevator and all the activity that takes place there. This will give you insight you've never had before. If you're ready, let's head out."

As they rode along lost in their own thoughts, Mr. Sellers broke the silence and asked, "Boys, have you ever had to negotiate the price of something?"

John answered, "Mr. Sellers, we've never even been to market, much less negotiated a price. However, one time I watched Dad negotiate a price for a plow. If I remember correctly, the seller wanted much more than Dad was willing to pay. The seller and Dad went back and forth several times, talking about what the plow was worth until finally the man got real mad and told Dad he was stealing the equipment from him. Dad paid him, and the man stormed off really angry. That's the only experience I've ever had. Chuck, have you ever been in a negotiation?" Chuck readily admitted he had not. He hadn't even been around for that incident with Dad and the man selling the farm equipment. He wondered where his dad had learned to negotiate like that.

Mr. Sellers drove on, and it was evident to the boys that he was thinking about what he would say next. They liked that about Mr.

43

Sellers. He didn't just blurt out whatever came to mind but thought carefully before he opened his mouth. "Boys, life is a lot like this road. It has bends and sometimes it's rough. Other times it's smooth and straight with very few hills or valleys. When it comes to negotiations of any kind, it's important to understand that the parties are looking at matters from the perspective of their life's road at the time, and in most cases, their roads are very different. For instance, you may be in a season of life where your road is straight and smooth while the person you are negotiating with may be in a season of rough roads. Your smooth road may make it easier for you to have patience and understanding while the person on a rough road may be desperate and not very yielding.

"When you're negotiating, it's important that you understand what kind of road you're traveling at the time. It's never a good idea to negotiate from a point of desperation. Keep a clear head about you, not allowing emotion to skew what you perceive to be the value of what you're buying or selling. This is the best position to work from. If you've made good choices, likely you'll be in a good position to negotiate. If you've made poor choices, you may find yourself desperate and not able to negotiate your best deal. Your goal is to keep your road as smooth and straight as possible. Before you seal a deal, ask yourself: Is this decision going to help me keep my road straight and calm, or is it going to cause me to have a rough patch? If you can't leave that negotiation knowing you've done all you could to keep your road straight, then you haven't negotiated effectively. Does that make sense?"

Chuck, admittedly, was confused. "I don't understand how your life's circumstances affect establishment of a price . . ."

John, who had been thinking about Mr. Sellers's words in light of the negotiation he had witnessed with his father, interrupted, "Do you suppose the man selling the farm equipment was angry with Dad because he was negotiating from a position of weakness and was desperate?"

Mr. Sellers smiled slightly and replied, "Well, I wasn't there, so it would be hard for me to say for sure. However, it is possible. Sometimes people purchase things, become attached to them, and then, when they are desperate for money, they try to sell them for what they think they are worth. The problem is, their desperation has brought their emotions into the process, and what they think an object is worth may or may not be an accurate value at all. Remember, things are just things. Their value is based in what someone is willing to pay for them. This is hard for people to accept, because they think the value of their thing is higher simply because they value it.

"When we arrive at market, Mr. Hillman is going to tell us what he is willing to pay for the cottonseed. We will have to measure if the offer he is giving us is worth the amount of effort you boys and I put into that crop and the total outlay we've put into buying the initial seed, the manpower, and the equipment we've expended to plant and harvest. Will we make a profit at the price he is offering? His offer is an indication of what our labor was worth. Now, if we think the value of our labor is greater than what he is offering—not taking into account the market conditions—we could opt to hold on to the crop while we look for another buyer. I've done this before. In some cases, this has caused me to lose money because another buyer didn't necessarily offer as much. There are a lot of factors you must weigh when you consider an offer to determine if it is reasonable."

Both Chuck and John were trying to understand the points being made. Mr. Sellers could see they were having a hard time fully grasping the concepts, and so he assured them, "You'll have a much better understanding of all of this after participating in the transaction with Mr. Hillman today. I'll be there to help, but I want you boys to take the lead in this negotiation.

"When you're trying to agree on a price, there is a second key to negotiation you must remember. You need to strike a mutually beneficial deal. Some people will push until they feel the other party has lost in the transaction. How likely do you think someone is going to be to enter into negotiation with the same person again if they feel like they always come out on the losing end of every transaction?"

Chuck was quick to answer, "If I was made to feel like a loser, you wouldn't see me coming around looking for another chance to get trounced!"

"Exactly, Chuck." Mr. Sellers continued, "Typically, the win-lose style of negotiation results in only a single transaction between the parties, as most people don't like being on the losing end. The ideal scenario is one in which you get a fair price while the other party gets a fair deal too. That kind of negotiation insures that the next time you have something to sell, you'll have someone interested, because they know they'll get a fair deal. Mr. Hillman and I have done business together for over twenty years. We both understand the other has a job to do as we negotiate pricing, so we always look to strike a deal that is beneficial to us both. If I had been unreasonable in my demands to the point that he made a poor decision and lost money, I would likely not have a buyer for our crops the next time I went to market. Equally, if he had insisted on paying a price that was so low I could not make money, he would definitely lose my business when the next crop came in. Does this make a little more sense?"

Both of the boys nodded their heads in understanding. Mr. Sellers continued, "Now listen, boys, I want you to know I had a conversation with Mr. Hillman regarding your quest for knowledge and understanding. He was very intrigued about the project we've undertaken and has been impressed with your commitment and diligence with this harvest. He has expressed a willingness to spend some time showing you his operations. I think this is a great opportunity for you. Hillman is well respected and has turned his company around from near bankruptcy to extreme profitability. As a matter of fact, at this point, the only one in the company with more authority than Hillman is the president himself. With all he's done to turn around that failing company, I'm sure he'll have some good points to make to help you boys turn around the direction of your family."

Mr. Sellers and the brothers pulled into the parking area in front of the grain elevator office. Towering above the office was the elevator itself. The boys had never seen such a sight—the elevator was so tall, it seemed to reach all the way to heaven, blocking the sun from shining on the spot of land where they were standing. Railroad cars spanned one long side of the complex, ready to be filled with grain for transport to other areas of the country. Wagons were lined up approaching the elevator itself, each waiting its turn to unload its precious cargo. It seemed like there were people everywhere. There were farmers standing visiting with each other; there were men with clipboards counting and shouting directions; and there were men working to unload the wagons that had made it to the front of the line by the elevator. The whole scene reminded Chuck of the anthills he'd observed as a kid. On those anthills, the ants all moved with purpose, like they had someplace very important to get to and no one had better stand in their way. Here at the grain elevator, it seemed like there were hundreds of people, all working together to get shipments offloaded and stored away.

Mr. Sellers led the boys up the steps onto the long porch in front of the elevator offices. On the left, they saw a sign over the door that read "Seller Registration." At the opposite end of the long porch, there was a sign over a door that read "Buyers Desk and Shipping." Mr. Sellers grabbed the handle and entered the Seller Registration office.

As they approached the registration desk, a voice called out, "Mr. Sellers, fancy seeing you on cotton day. I thought you only came on wheat days."

The boys looked in the direction of the voice as Mr. Sellers replied, "Well, Margaret, sometimes an old dog learns new tricks. But mostly, I couldn't wait to see you again."

Margaret, a plump woman with stringy brown hair heaped haphazardly on top of her head, looked at Mr. Sellers with skepticism. Then a smile broke out over her face and she said, "Flattery will get you everywhere, Mr. Sellers. I suppose you want to see Mr. Hillman and get current pricing for cotton."

With a twinkle in his eye, Mr. Sellers replied, "If you don't mind."

Though her words were addressed to Mr. Sellers, Margaret had not taken her eye off Chuck and John since they stepped into the small office. "For you, anything. But tell me, who are the young men with you?" Maybe the woman was just being nosy or maybe she was doing her job, sizing up the boys to decide if they had any business being in her office.

Mr. Sellers didn't seem offended by the question. "These are two of my best men, protégés of sorts. I'm going to introduce them to Mr. Hillman today."

"Let's see how that goes. He is in quite a mood today. Something about the bins. He's been muttering about it all day. Here are your pricing sheets. Be aware, the last guy who was here didn't get what he wanted and left. It was quite a scene. Here comes Mr. Hillman now."

"Thanks for the warning, Margaret," said Mr. Sellers. Just as the men turned, they saw Mr. Hillman walking up. As was his custom, Hillman was dressed impeccably in suit pants, a crisp white shirt, dark vest, and matching tie. Not a hair was out of place, even in the midst of what the boys imagined must be for him a very demanding day. From first glance, the boys were struck by his professionalism.

"Mr. Sellers, so good to see you. And this must be Chuck and John. Good to meet you boys. Mr. Sellers has told me a lot about you."

"Good to see you as well, my old friend," Sellers said warmly. "Margaret has already warned me you're in a great mood and paying double market price today." He followed that comment with a hearty laugh.

"Good old Margaret. With her promising prices like that, I can count on a quick dispatch to the poor house."

Margaret interrupted, "Promising prices like that, I can count on Mr. Sellers marrying me."

Everyone enjoyed a good laugh, and then Mr. Hillman said, "Let's go see what you've brought me."

Mr. Sellers led the group to his wagons that were still waiting their turn in line. At the gin, the cottonseed had been dried and placed into bags for transport to the elevator. Mr. Hillman now opened up one of the bags to inspect the cottonseed. "Looks like you brought in an impressive harvest, gentlemen, and the seed is high quality. What were you looking to make from the sale of your seed today?"

Chuck looked at John, hoping he'd throw out the first number. It was soon obvious that John wouldn't be speaking first—he looked like a frightened animal—so Chuck dove in. "Well, Mr. Hillman, I don't know how much Mr. Sellers has told you about my brother and me, but we're new to the world of business. We tried to do some checking on the going price for cottonseed before we came up here today and what we found is that seed is going for around two cents per pound, or thirty-six dollars and forty-one cents a ton."

"You are correct, Chuck. That's the wholesale price our elevator is currently asking for cottonseed. But you're not looking to buy, you're looking to sell your seed. Surely you understand that I cannot pay you what I'm asking for the seed myself. I have to allow myself enough profit margin to cover the expenses I will incur to store the seed and distribute it to those who wish to purchase it on down the road. So with that in mind, let's think about what might be a fair price for the seed you've brought me today. Since this is your first business negotiation, let me throw out the first number. I would feel comfortable paying you one point four cents per pound, or twenty-eight dollars a ton."

Mr. Sellers smiled as he watched the brothers' fledgling efforts at negotiation. After Hillman made his opening offer, he saw the pleading look in Chuck's eye and knew it was a cry for help. "That's a fair offer, Hillman. John, Chuck, how do you feel about that offer?"

"Well, I agree that is a fair opening offer, Mr. Hillman," said John, "but is there room for any increase? I know it certainly cost our farm a pretty penny in labor and materials to plant and harvest this cotton. If we could get maybe one point eight cents per pound, I'd sure feel a lot better."

Mr. Hillman stared off into the distance for a moment, obviously doing the calculations in his mind. "I don't know that I could go as high as one point eight cents per pound, but based on the quality of the seed you've brought me, I believe I'd be comfortable paying you one point six cents per pound, or thirty-two dollars per ton. Do we have a deal, gentlemen?"

The brothers looked at Mr. Sellers and saw him nod in assent. "Yes, sir, I think we would be happy selling to you at that price point," said John.

"Excellent. Now before we head back to the office to write up the paperwork, I have one more question for you boys. You've got an abundance of cottonseed here. Are you wanting to sell all of this, or are you wanting to hold back some of this seed for your next planting?"

The boys looked to Mr. Sellers, expecting him to answer Mr. Hillman's question, but Mr. Sellers did not reply. Instead, he looked back at the boys and said, "Yes, boys, how much of this seed are you wanting to sell today and how much are you wanting to hold back for your next planting?"

"We . . . well . . . we really hadn't thought about that," John replied.

"This is something you have to consider, boys," said Mr. Sellers. "When we decided to plant cotton this first time, I had to purchase seven hundred and fifty pounds of seed to plant the acreage we'd devoted to cotton. That cost me money out of pocket. Here you sit with bags full of seed. Of course, you'll want to sell the majority, but it would make sense for you to hold some back to put in the ground to raise your next cotton crop when the season comes."

"How much should we hold back, Mr. Sellers?"

"Mr. Hillman, I think I'll let you field that question. Boys, Mr. Hillman's wisdom in this area far exceeds my own. I've learned a thing or two from him over the years and now you'll get to benefit from his wisdom, just as I have."

"Mr. Sellers, your kind words mean the world to me. I cannot take credit for any wisdom I may have. God has been a faithful teacher to me over the years when I've turned to him for guidance and direction. His Word has been a guide, even in the area of business. Boys, have you spent much time reading the Bible?"

The boys admitted that though their father read the Bible every night, they had not developed that habit. They didn't even own a copy themselves, having not seen it as very important to their daily lives as farmhands. They consulted the *Farmers' Almanac* regularly, but not the Bible. Chuck asked the question they both had in mind: "Mr. Hillman, no offense, but what could the Bible possibly have to say about farming?"

"More than you might imagine, Chuck. For instance, you know how Mr. Sellers makes a practice of letting a field rest after it has been planted for a number of years? That plan is laid out in the Bible. God created the soil and he knows it needs some time to replenish after crops have taken minerals from it for a few years. That is why he provided for a sabbath year, for the land to rest every seventh year. This is good for the soil, and ensures that in the other six years, the crops will flourish."

"But how can the Bible help us guess how much seed we should hold back from this year's crop? Surely it doesn't get that specific," said John.

"You're right, John, it's not quite that specific, but the Bible does serve as a guide to help you understand how to balance what you sell or spend with what you hold back for the future. A good rule of thumb is to save at least twenty percent of what you bring in, and live on the other eighty percent. If you'll do that, you'll have plenty for today and won't have to worry about tomorrow, because you'll know you've prepared for contingencies. Does that make sense?"

Chuck and John had to admit that they'd never considered saving for the future. Their family had always lived hand to mouth, just making enough to cover their modest expenses. The thought of putting anything aside for the future was almost more than they could grasp. "So you're saying we should sell eighty percent of the seed that we have here and take twenty percent of it back to the farm with us?" John asked.

"That is completely up to you. I'm just sharing with you from lessons I've learned. When I first started working here at the grain elevator, the business was in trouble. As you've seen firsthand today, the way a grain elevator operates is, we receive grain from the farmers and pay a negotiated price for their crops. We then sell the grain to our customers—ranchers, mills, other farmers, and so on—with enough markup to cover our costs and return a small profit to the business. If we don't have enough money to buy the grain from the farmers in the first place, then we have nothing to sell, which means we'll have even less money the next time to buy grain and even less to sell. With those kinds of business practices, a grain elevator won't stay in business long. Unfortunately, that was exactly the cycle ownership had us in when I first came on. They'd made a habit of spending every penny they brought in either to pay the workers or to buy more grain in the next cycle. One year, they were caught off guard when the bottom dropped out of the market and they were unable to recoup the money they had spent purchasing grain from the farmers. Once they got behind, they just couldn't seem to catch up, mainly because they'd failed to plan for such an occurrence.

"The owners came to me one day and told me they were going to have to shut down the grain elevator. I asked them to give me one chance to turn things around. They agreed, and I got to work. The first thing I did was I started to save. I determined we would never be caught unprepared again. Though things were tough for a while and we had to let some of our workers go—men who had been with us for years—we stayed in business and diligently saved twenty percent of all the monies we brought in from the sale of the grain we'd purchased. Now here we are, eight years later and completely solvent. We work this plan every cycle, saving twenty percent and profiting on the other eighty percent of what we bring in. We've never let another employee go for financial reasons, and have actually been able to hire back every man we originally let go. This plan of saving can work, if you'll commit yourself to it."

"Joseph," said Mr. Sellers, "we've taken up enough of your time, and I know Chuck and John are going to need some time to digest what you've shared with us today. Boys, looks like our wagons are approaching the elevator. Let's watch them offload our seed."

"Sellers, before you go, may I share one more bit of advice with your young protégés? Perhaps the most important thing to remember as you're dealing with income is the importance of giving a bit away. I know that sounds contradictory, but it actually makes sense. When you give some of your income away, it reminds you to not hold on too tightly to things that are perishable. I know that every good and perfect thing I have came from God, including my ability to create wealth. I never want my possessions to have such a hold on me that I forget Who is most important. With the success you've had with this crop, you're probably going to experience a windfall unlike anything you've seen in the past. I hope this final bit of advice I've shared with you makes sense and that you'll give it the consideration it deserves. Now, I have taken enough of your time. I wish you gentlemen all the best. Good day."

Mr. Sellers and the boys walked over to their wagons. "All that Mr. Hillman told us makes good sense. Mr. Sellers, do you think we might be able to hold back twenty percent of the bags of seed we brought here today?" asked Chuck.

Mr. Sellers replied, "I think that sounds like a very wise decision on your part. John, are you in agreement with that?"

"I'd surely like to have the money that seed would bring in today, but I understand what Mr. Hillman was saying. I suppose it can't hurt to save back twenty percent of this seed and see what happens from there," said John.

"That final tidbit Mr. Hillman shared with you demands consideration," said Mr. Sellers. "It's very easy to grow attached to your money, your land, your livestock, to anything that gives you a sense of security—but all of those things can be gone in a minute. In the many years I've been farming, I've had good yields and bad yields. Some years, it's been a stretch to pay my farmhands. You can see how those kinds of worries could take a toll on a person. To maintain proper perspective, it's important that you hold on to things of this world loosely. Giving away a portion of your income and living on what's left reminds you that no matter how much or how little you have, it is ultimately God who takes care of you. Giving keeps your eyes focused on God, and not on things that can let you down."

*****

In one week, the boys had an appointment to meet with the representative from the cotton exchange to discuss what they would do with the cotton lint. Solomon Brady was expecting them, and the boys would be going farther away from home than they'd ever been to meet with him—they'd travel all the way to the state capital of Oklahoma City. But today, they'd cleared their first hurdle: the seed was sold.

Mr. Sellers asked the boys to join him in his office when they returned to the farm. Sitting behind his desk, he pulled out a stack of money and began counting out the boys' share from the sale of the seed. To their amazement, Mr. Sellers continued counting for quite some time.

Once the money had been counted out, Mr. Sellers pushed it across the desk to the brothers. "Have you boys given any thought to what you're going to do with this much money?"

It took John a minute to pry his jaw open, he was in such shock at the sight of that much money. He'd never seen so many bills laid in one place in his whole life. "Well, we certainly can't spend it all. What do you recommend we do, Mr. Sellers?"

"I'd recommend you pay a visit to Mr. Johnson at the bank in town. He can set up deposit accounts for you gentlemen, and, if you plan to heed the advice Mr. Hillman gave you—and I strongly recommend that you do—Johnson can also help you set up separate savings accounts to put back some of the money for the future."

"Johnson. Why does that name sound familiar?" asked Chuck.

"Johnson is also Reba's last name. The banker is her father."

"Oh, I see," said Chuck, but honestly he was confused. What was the daughter of the town banker doing working as a secretary and bookkeeper for a farmer? Her father had to be very wealthy— why was someone of Reba's means working at all? That girl was a mystery—one that he wouldn't mind trying to figure out.

CHAPTER 8

The next morning, Chuck and John headed out early so they could be at the bank when it opened for the day. Their route into town took them by a few neighboring farms. As they passed by the old Hughes place, they noticed a "For Sale" sign tacked to a tree. Chuck brought his horse to a halt and dismounted to take a better look at the property. Everyone knew everyone's business in Grady County, which was both a blessing and a curse, depending on how you looked at it. They knew that old man Hughes had some health problems and hadn't been able to keep up with his property as he should. The Hughes had never been able to have children, so they couldn't depend on family to help them out, and as the years passed, they'd had to give up altogether on planting any of their land. It looked like the parcel that was posted for sale hadn't been tended to in a very long time.

"What are you looking at, Chuck?"

"Did you know old man Hughes had put this parcel up for sale? I wonder what he's asking for it."

"What does it matter what he's asking for it? I'm sure it's more than what we've got in our pockets right now. We need to get to town when the bank opens, because after we finish up our business there, we still have a full day of chores back at the farm waiting on us. Let's be on our way, Chuck."

"I wasn't implying that we have enough money in our pockets to plunk down on the table to buy this land right now, John, but you know we are going to be bringing in some more money once we dispose of the cotton lint. Depending on what Mr. Hughes is asking, we may be able to swing this. Could you imagine owning your own land, brother? I'm going to ask Mr. Johnson if he knows anything about the asking price for this property."

"Well, you'll only be able to ask him if we actually make it to the bank, so let's go."

*****

As the brothers walked into the bank that morning, they didn't know what to expect. What they found were friendly people who seemed willing to help. "Excuse me, we were looking to speak with Mr. Johnson, if we could," John said to the first person he met through the door.

The bank teller smiled and said, "But of course. Who may I tell him is calling?"

"My name is John Kindig and this is my brother, Chuck. We work for Mr. Sellers. He sent us."

"Oh! Mr. Sellers is an excellent man. I'm sure Mr. Johnson will want to visit with any employees of his. Let me see if he's free." The teller walked down the hall, and when he returned, he opened up the swinging gate and invited the boys to follow him to Mr. Johnson's office.

The banker's office was large, with windows overlooking the town square. Mr. Johnson stood to shake hands with the brothers, inviting them to be seated in the chairs in front of his desk before returning to his own seat. "So, you're employees of Mr. Sellers, I hear. Have you had occasion to meet my daughter, Reba? She works in the office there on the farm."

"We have had the pleasure to meet Miss Reba in the office. She's always been very helpful," said John.

"She does enjoy her work out at the farm," Mr. Johnson said. "So what brings you to my savings and loan today, gentlemen? How can I be of service?"

"We have some money, and since the amount is more than we've ever had in our possession before, we thought it might be best to make inquiries at the bank to see about locking it in a safe or something," said Chuck.

"Though how my clients come to possess their money is usually none of my business, since you have stated you are employees of Sellers and acquaintances of my daughter, I feel a certain right to be a bit more nosy than I might usually be. How did you boys come to be in possession of such a large sum that you'd think to entrust it to a bank for safekeeping?"

"Well, sir, our boss Mr. Sellers gave us a great opportunity to work a field from start to finish ourselves. We had asked him some questions about success and he seemed to think that the best way to learn what it takes to be successful is to actually have some hands-on experience. So we prepared a field, planted it with cotton, supervised and worked alongside a crew that tended the field, and when the harvest was taken in, it turned out we'd reaped far and away more than we or Mr. Sellers had ever dreamed we would. Mr. Sellers graciously offered to split the profits of the sale of the crop with us. We accompanied him to have the cotton ginned, to sell the seed at the grain elevator, and in just a few days, we'll be traveling to Oklahoma City to visit with the head of the cotton cooperative about what we plan to do with the lint. We have our portion of the money from the sale of the seed in our pockets right now. That is what we'd like to lock away in your safe. Once we've decided what to do with the lint, we'll probably be back to lock away a little more."

Mr. Johnson paused for a moment and then a smile broke across his face. "Sounds like you boys have had quite a start to your career in farming. My daughter mentioned this arrangement Sellers had with some of his men. I guess you two are the men to whom she was referring. Of course we'd be more than happy to open an account for you here at our bank. If you'll give me just one moment, I'll have one of my tellers join us and we'll complete the paperwork."

"Mr. Johnson, could I ask you just one more question?" said Chuck.

"Certainly, you can feel free to ask anything."

"What do you know about the parcel of land the Hughes family has posted for sale? Do you know how much acreage they're offering and what the asking price might be?"

"Actually, I do," said Mr. Johnson. "The Hughes family is offering sixty acres for sale at the price of fifty-two dollars per acre, which is actually a very fair price for this county. Now, I know that the land they're offering hasn't been worked for a very, very long time, so there is a chance a good negotiator could get the parcel for a little less, but that's what they're asking right now. If you don't have any additional questions, please excuse me while I get the teller."

When Johnson left the room, Chuck turned to John. "I think we could swing that! Not right now, of course, but once we sell our cotton lint, I actually think there's a good chance we could purchase those sixty acres, especially if we could negotiate the price down just a bit. We could be landowners, John!"

*****

Mr. Sellers had laid out three options to the brothers for what they could to do with their cotton lint. The first option was they could sell all the lint directly to a textile mill in Texas. If they chose this option, they would see their profits immediately, but being a relatively small farm, they did not have much bargaining power, so they might not get the best price per pound.

Option number two provided for the boys to keep all of the cotton in storage and borrow money against it. This, too, gave them immediate income, but was the riskiest of the three options. If the bottom fell out of the cotton market, the boys could find themselves owing more to the bank than what their storehouse full of cotton was worth.

The third option involved entrusting all of the lint to the cotton cooperative in Oklahoma City. The cotton cooperative would pay the brothers a portion of what their crop was worth upon delivery at their warehouses. The cooperative would then negotiate with one of the big textile mills located around the country for sale of the boys' cotton combined with cotton from all the other cooperative members in the state. Because the cooperative negotiated bigger sales on behalf of all of their members, chances were the boys would receive a higher price per pound for their cotton through the cooperative.

Once the sale of the cotton was finalized, the boys would receive the remainder of their profits, less the cooperative's fee for service.

After careful consideration, the boys determined they would entrust their crop to the cotton cooperative, and so today, they were off to Oklahoma City to meet with Solomon Brady, the head of the state's cooperative. Their cotton lint was traveling ahead of them by rail car to the cooperative's storage facility. Mr. Sellers and the boys were heading to Oklahoma City in his automobile.

The boys enjoyed these rides with Mr. Sellers. No one in their family had ever owned a car, so travel by automobile was still a novelty to them. As it would happen, they had plenty of time to enjoy themselves. The trip to Oklahoma City covered just over sixty miles, but with Mr. Sellers insisting on remaining well under the maximum posted highway speed of thirty-five miles per hour, the trip took the better part of the morning. As the car bumped along the road headed north to the city, Mr. Sellers asked, "What are you most interested in seeing when we're in the state capital over these next few days?"

Chuck was the first to speak up. "I want to see everything! I've never been to a big city before so I want to see everything!"

John replied, "You'd better take it in now, brother. No telling if we'll ever get back to the city again."

"How can you even say that? With all we've learned so far, we're destined for bigger things than just a life on the farm."

The car suddenly went silent. "I'm sorry, Mr. Sellers. I meant no disrespect. You know I admire you and respect all you've done with your land. You're the most successful man I know. I just mean I don't want to live the rest of my life working in the fields like so many of my people before me have done. I want to do better for myself so I can leave something behind for my family."

Mr. Sellers chuckled. "I'm not the least bit offended. I know you meant no disrespect, Chuck. The desire to better yourself is a healthy one. I hope you've been taking in everything the men you've met so far have told you. There's a verse in the Bible that says if you want to be wise, you should walk with the wise. Boys, you've been walking with the wise lately. If you've gathered the wisdom they've laid out in front of you, you're definitely wiser than when you started your quest.

"Our first order of business is to meet with Mr. Solomon Brady. I've never met him myself, but Joseph Hillman knows him from a professional association and is impressed with him. I'll warn you boys, you'll be tempted to let the sights and sounds of the big city distract you. You need to decide now that you're not here as sightseers, you're here as businessmen intent on striking a deal for the sale of your cotton, and if you can pick up some wisdom in the process, that's even better."

Oklahoma City was the busiest place the brothers had ever seen. There were cars everywhere and the buildings were huge. As the car pulled up in front of the hotel, Chuck could not believe his eyes. "I think this place is even taller than the grain elevator in Chickasha! How do they build buildings so tall?"

They unloaded their satchels and walked into the lobby of the hotel. "Shut your mouth, Chuck. You're catching flies," John teased, but the older brother was just as impressed. The farm had limited electrical service, which meant that the bunkhouse was still lit by oil lamps. The electric lights in this town made it seem like the brightest place on earth. The men settled in their room and washed up, then headed over to the cooperative offices to meet Mr. Brady.

The cooperative was located in the industrial section of the city. Rail cars were lined up at loading docks alongside warehouses that seemed to stretch for miles. Mr. Sellers and the boys pushed through the door into the front office of the cooperative. A young lady sat at a small desk with a plate on the front that read "Receptionist." She had a pleasant face and warm smile as she greeted the men and asked how she could be of service. "We're here to see Solomon Brady. We have an appointment. The name is Sellers."

"Oh, yes, Mr. Sellers. Mr. Brady is expecting you. Let me ring him." The young lady picked up her telephone and dialed. "Mr. Brady? Mr. Sellers and his associates are here for your two p.m. appointment. Yes, sir. I'll bring them right back."

The receptionist hung up the phone and rose from her desk, asking the men to follow her to Mr. Brady's office. She was dressed in the flapper style of the day. John couldn't help but think as he followed the young lady that they were a long way from the farm. Other than when they managed to make it to church, the boys didn't have much interaction with members of the fairer sex. The only women they saw on a semi-regular basis were their mother and Reba, Mr. Sellers's assistant. Reba dressed more modern than their mother ever had, but still she was conservative compared to this woman. What would his mother think if she saw this getup?

Mr. Brady greeted the men and asked them to have a seat. He sat behind a large desk—one much larger than either Mr. Sellers's desk back at the farm or even Mr. Johnson's desk at the bank. Like in Mr. Sellers's office and Mr. Johnson's office, there was a big window. Maybe it was a requirement that all important men have windows in their offices. The window in this office was behind Mr. Brady's desk and looked out over the city. Mr. Brady was dressed in a dark suit with a crisp white shirt and nice necktie. The boys could immediately see why Mr. Hillman respected this man. He had an air of authority about him, and they couldn't help but notice that the two men shared the same affinity for dark suits and blindingly white shirts.

"Gentlemen, I am so glad you've decided to join our little cooperative. When Joseph called to visit with me about you, I must say I was impressed by your story. You seem like men of ambition. And Mr. Sellers, I must commend you as well. Your life evidences an understanding of the truth that in order for a spring to remain fresh, it must have water flowing both in and out of it. I admire the investment you're making in these young men. You surely will be blessed for your efforts. Now what questions can I answer for you?"

Mr. Sellers began, "Mr. Hillman has told you about our little venture into raising cotton. We've been strictly a wheat farm for many years, but knew we needed to diversify a bit, so we planted a field with cotton. We had a bumper crop the first time out, thanks to the diligence of John and Chuck. We've had the cotton ginned, have sold off a portion of the seed, and now we are here to dispose of our cotton lint. I've explained to John and Chuck what our options are for the lint, and we've already had it shipped here to your warehouses by train. I'm certain it arrived in advance of us."

"Yes, it has arrived. I noticed an entry for your cotton on the daily inventory report I received this morning. For only having planted limited acreage, your yield was outstanding. Now we come to the question of what you want to do with the lint. Obviously, you've ruled out selling to a textile mill yourselves. That's a wise choice. Our members receive consistently higher prices per pound for their cotton because of our strong negotiating power as a cooperative, if selling is the direction you intend to go. You also have the option of leaving your cotton in storage here at our secure warehouses and using it as collateral for a loan. We can help you negotiate a fair interest rate and you can return to your farm with money in hand."

Mr. Sellers looked at John and Chuck and, though he had laid out these options to the boys earlier, he felt he should give them just a bit more explanation about the option of borrowing against their crop to stress to them the possible risks involved in making such a choice. "John, Chuck, if you opt to take out a loan against the value of your cotton, you would sign a promissory note. That note is a legal document that says you agree to pay back over time every cent the cooperative gives you, plus interest. If you fail to make the agreed-upon payments, you forfeit your cotton to the cooperative."

"That is correct, Mr. Sellers," said Mr. Brady. "If you gentlemen wish to take out a loan against the value of your cotton, you'll leave the city with the full market value of your cotton in hand. Once you've paid off the balance of the promissory note, plus storage fees to the cooperative, the cotton will be yours free and clear, and you can do with it what you'd like at that time."

"So we could get money for the cotton now and later?" asked Chuck. All Chuck could think of was the "For Sale" sign they'd seen on that parcel of land. If they had the full value of their lint in hand when they went home, there was no question that they'd be able to purchase the land for themselves before someone else snatched it up.

Mr. Brady spoke and woke Chuck from his daydream about land ownership. "In a way you could have money now and later, but remember, the money you would receive now you would have to pay back, with interest, and you'd be incurring storage fees. Only after you'd paid off the note would the cotton fully belong to you again so you could sell it. There's always a risk with borrowing money. Who knows what the value of your cotton might be a few years from now when you pay off that note? We fully expect the price of cotton to continue to rise, but we cannot guarantee it."

"I just don't know how a man decides what to do. Seems like it's a risk any way you look at it," said John.

"Matters of business require great wisdom. In fact, I can't think of a more important asset a businessman can possess than wisdom. When I was asked to head up this cooperative, I didn't know if I had the skills necessary to make it a success. I fully understood that the livelihood of farmers all throughout this state would be resting on my shoulders. If I failed to negotiate good prices for their cotton, families and workers would suffer. For some smaller farms, the deals I'm able to strike mean the difference between another year of planting and going under. Thoughts about this reality almost led me to decline the position, and I still feel the weight of the responsibility every day that I come into this office.

"Do you mind if I ask you gentlemen a personal question?"

John replied for the group: "Not at all, Mr. Brady. Ask anything you'd like."

"Are you men of faith? What I mean is, do you have faith that there is a God you can come to with your thoughts, your petitions, your anxieties, and do you believe God cares about you and what concerns you?"

After a moment of silence, Chuck replied, "Yes, sir, I would say that I do. Throughout my life, I watched my dad read his Bible, and I always knew church was important to him. Before my brother and I first talked to Mr. Sellers about our quest for knowledge and understanding of the ways of success, I prayed that God would grant us favor with Mr. Sellers. Honestly, when I first prayed that prayer, I wasn't sure if God could hear me or if he even cared about my request. But when Mr. Sellers agreed to help us, I guess that made me think that maybe my prayers did matter to God. I've found myself praying more and more these days. I suppose that means that I do believe that God hears what I'm saying and he cares."

John nodded a few times in agreement but never spoke up. Of course he believed in God. Who didn't? But the jury was still out for him on whether or not God really sought to make a difference in his everyday life. I mean, there had been a fifty-fifty chance Mr. Sellers was going to help them when they asked. Did God care enough to intervene in something that was a good possibility anyway? He just couldn't say that he was sure either way.

"Chuck, that's a perfect way of describing the establishment of a walk of faith," said Mr. Brady. "You prayed and trusted God to hear and answer your prayer. Then you took action. If I understood you correctly, you'd say that the more you've done that, the stronger your faith in God has become, correct?"

"Yes, sir. That's exactly how it's been."

"And so it was with me. When I agreed to accept the position as head of this cooperative, I prayed and asked God for wisdom. I prayed fervently, like the success or failure of this entire venture depended on God hearing and answering my prayer. But then I actually had to come into the office and do the work. I had to study the market trends and establish the relationships with the textile mills. I had to recruit members into the cooperative. I had to negotiate the prices with the mills and oversee the logistics of getting lint to buyer. I worked hard, like it all depended on me; but at the same time, I also prayed like it all depended on God. I think the success of the cooperative speaks to the success of that model. God has, indeed, answered my prayer for wisdom. I have been able to clearly see market trends, and doors have opened to me that have benefitted all of our members. But I had to have the courage and fortitude to do the daily work. If I could impress one thing upon your memory, it would be this lesson. Pray like it all depends on God and work like it all depends on you."

Now it was John's turn to speak. "Mr. Brady, I think that's exactly what we did with this cotton crop. We prayed every day over this cotton. We prayed for rain, we prayed the weevils would stay away, we prayed for clear skies during harvest. Seems like all we did was pray and work, and things seem to have turned out well."

"You've got a good handle on what I'm saying, John. But understand that you can ask God for more than just physical provision like rain or clear skies. The eternal, omniscient God can also give you those intangibles you so desperately need for success, things like wisdom and peace and patience. The higher you climb on the ladder of success, the more you're going to need these things every single day. Trust me on that one.

"Now, to the question before us. What do you want to do with your cotton lint? You now understand the process involved with putting up your lint as collateral for a loan. We have the paperwork here to facilitate that, and you can leave today with money in hand. Should you choose to go the other direction and offer your lint for sale in combination with lint from all our other cooperative members, I'll have you sign a contract to that effect, and you'll leave here today with money in hand representing one-third of the current market value of the lint you've sent to our warehouses. Once we've finalized negotiations with the textile mill, you'll receive the other two-thirds of the negotiated value of your lint. Before I hear your decision, do you have any questions about the options before you?"

"I think you've explained our options quite clearly, Mr. Brady," Mr. Sellers said. "Could we have the night to think on this and discuss it amongst ourselves and then get back to you first thing in the morning with our decision?"

"Absolutely. I'll expect to hear from you bright and early tomorrow."

*****

"So, boys, you understand your options and the benefits and risks involved in each. What are your thoughts?"

"Well, Mr. Sellers, we were hoping you might decide for us, since whatever we decide affects you too, as our partner," said Chuck.

"No, gentlemen, this decision is on your shoulders. I'm here to act as a sounding board and give any advice I can, but, ultimately, I'm leaving the decision up to you."

"The way I see it, if we take out a loan on the value of the cotton, we get money now, and later. That seems like an incredible deal and you know what we could buy with that money, John. Then we'd just pay the money back once our next crop comes in. How could we go wrong? Mr. Sellers, do you agree?"

"Well, Chuck, I'd say it depends," began Mr. Sellers. "What are you planning to do with the money you're bringing in? Are you going to buy something that will have lasting value like land, or were you planning to buy something that may or may not have value down the road, like seed that once planted, may or may not result in a bountiful harvest? I've always believed that a person should only borrow money in those rare instances when the loan is almost guaranteed to work for them. You should never borrow for convenience's sake. If you can wait until you have cash in hand to make a purchase, it's always best to do so.

"There's one thing I've learned about borrowing money—the borrower is always slave to the lender. When you were raising your cotton crop, you knew that whatever came up out of the ground, you would benefit from it. It was all yours. That won't be the case with future crops if you opt to take a loan against this cotton. The bank will demand their money off the top.

"Think back to our conversation the very first time we went to see Mr. Hillman. Remember our talk about negotiation and how some people's ability to negotiate is affected by their circumstances. Some folks get themselves backed into a corner by decisions they've made, and that affects their ability to negotiate effectively. It also robs them of their peace. If you take a loan against the value of this crop, you'll have to make certain you get at least as much for your next crop as you received in a loan this time, otherwise you'll have a hard time paying that money back and your master—the bank—is not a forgiving taskmaster. What happens if the weather doesn't cooperate or if the cotton market fluctuates? Will you be able to negotiate effectively with Mr. Hillman for the price of seed or with Mr. Brady for the value of your lint the next time you go to market? Or will decisions you make today put a strain on you and cloud your judgment? Will the decisions you make today make it easier or harder for you to sleep tomorrow night? That's what you have to ask yourself."

"Chuck, I think it's clear. We should entrust the lint to Mr. Brady and the cooperative to sell for us. I know that means we won't have as much money in hand right away, but we don't need cash on hand right now. I say we allow Mr. Brady to sell the lint and then once we have the full value of the crop in hand, we can decide our next move at that time. That seems like the wisest course of action. What say you, brother?"

Chuck had to agree that Mr. Sellers's words made sense. As did John's. They didn't need cash in hand right then. They had good jobs and plenty of time to wait for fortune to come their way. "I agree, John. Tomorrow, we'll tell Mr. Brady we'd like to have him sell our lint and then we'll see how much we end up with after all is said and done."

CHAPTER 9

John and Chuck returned to the farm from Oklahoma City, and the next day, made another trip to the bank to deposit the down payment they had received for their lint. On the way to the bank, Chuck made certain they rode by the Hughes place. He almost whooped when he saw that the "For Sale" sign was still on the tree. The place might just belong to them yet.

Week after week, Chuck would find some excuse to ride by the Hughes farm, and each time he saw the sign still on the tree, he would let out a sigh of relief. It was fair to say that Chuck was obsessed with the idea of purchasing that land.

On a Wednesday afternoon, the boys were out mending fence on the property line when Mr. Sellers rode out to them. "Boys, I've just heard from the cooperative. Our lint has been sold and the remaining balance due us has been wired to my account. Tomorrow, we'll head over to town and have your shares moved from my account to yours."

They would finally have money in hand! Of course, all that Chuck wanted to know was whether they were too late to purchase what he'd come to think of as "their" farm. "Mr. Sellers, do you have just a minute to talk to us?"

"Of course, Chuck. What's on your mind?"

"We've noticed that the Hughes family has a parcel of land posted for sale up the road. I've made some inquiries to see what they might be asking for the land, and John and I have discussed the matter. Now that we'll have money in hand from the sale of our lint, added to what we made from the sale of the seed, we were thinking that we might be interested in making an offer to purchase that property. I wanted to know your opinion."

Sellers took some time before he answered. He hated to lose two good hands, but he knew he had to put his own feelings aside and give the boys his honest opinion. "Gentlemen, I'd be lying if I said I'm OK with losing two of my best farmhands, but I'm a firm believer in following the path that God lays out for us, and if that path is taking you out on your own, then you must go.

"But with that said, let me give you this advice. When you are considering going out on your own, you would do well to remember all the lessons you've learned so far in your journey. Don't pay so much to go out on your own that you can't still put some back for the future. Don't overextend yourself so far that you can't give to others. You need to count the cost and see if such a purchase is feasible for you right now. Remember that if you go into something unprepared, you'll end up plagued with anxiety down the road, and anxiety leads to poor decisions. Only when you are diligent will you live in peace. If, after weighing the situation, you feel that purchasing the Hughes land is what's best, then know that you will have my full support."

"Mr. Sellers, thank you so much," said John. "We most definitely will remember all we've learned so far as we consider our next steps. I suppose the first thing we need to do is see if we can get the property for a price we're comfortable paying. Looks like it's time to negotiate again."

*****

"Well, gentlemen, that takes care of the transfer of funds between Mr. Sellers's account and your own. Congratulations on the sale of your lint. You had a very profitable season. Is there anything else I can do for you while you're here today?" asked Mr. Johnson.

"As a matter of fact, there is. If you'll recall, we'd asked previously about the old Hughes place that was posted for sale. When we came to town today, we noticed that the sign indicates the property is still available."

"Yes, Chuck. The property is still for sale," said Mr. Johnson.

"My brother and I are interested in making an offer to purchase the place," said Chuck. "You'd told us that the Hughes family was asking fifty-two dollars an acre. Because the land has been neglected for so long and the house on the property is in bad shape, not to mention there is no barn, we were thinking that a fair price might be closer to forty-eight dollars an acre. How might we go about seeing if that number is acceptable?"

"I do not believe the Hughes family has enlisted the help of any professionals to assist with the sales transaction, so you might start by talking to Mr. and Mrs. Hughes directly to settle on a fair price. If I can be of any help to you boys along the way, just let me know."

"Thank you, Mr. Johnson. You've been a big help. Hopefully the next time we see you, we'll be landowners."

*****

As John and Chuck surveyed the land, they thought to themselves that it was the most beautiful piece of property they'd ever seen in their lives. Beautiful, because the deed in their hands said it was theirs. They were glad they'd decided to wait on the money and allow Mr. Brady to sell their lint through the cooperative. They'd received a fair price for their cotton lint, and after some negotiation with Mr. and Mrs. Hughes over the price of the land, it turned out their cut of the profits gave them enough money to purchase this small parcel and still put some money in savings for the future.

No, they weren't looking at neatly tilled soil. In fact, the ground was uneven and looked as raw as the day God created it. There were some rocks, but the boys had strong backs and even stronger work ethics. They'd get rid of those rocks. There was no fence; the only objects of demarcation were some stakes driven into the ground at the four corners of the property. But the boys had built fences before and they would do so again here. For the first time in their family history, two of their own had risen above being tenant farmers. As John and Chuck looked down at the title deed, their vision blurred and they couldn't stop the flow of tears from their eyes. They were landowners. They so wished their dad was standing here with them now.

The boys would readily admit the place had some negatives. The main house would need some work. Actually, it was only a "house" in the most generous definition of the word. There were four walls and a roof and it was used as a residence—currently by possums or raccoons or some other family of critters. Once the boys replaced a few boards and gave the place a good cleaning, it would be their castle. There was no barn on the property, a fact they'd have to rectify quickly. Mr. Sellers had graciously promised them one of his old but reliable plows as a gift upon closing on the purchase of the land, but the boys had no animal to pull the plow, as of yet. "Minor details," Chuck said aloud, as he and John walked around making mental notes of which projects they'd be taking on first.

*****

The boys were grateful for the kindness of friends. A neighboring farmer had agreed to let them borrow his wagon and horse to go by Mr. Sellers's property to pick up the promised plow that day. As Chuck drove the wagon up toward the barn and offices, he was pleased to see Reba standing outside. She was looking down at a ledger book, and with the angle her head was tilted, the early morning sunlight made her red hair shine like copper. "Good morning, Chuck, John," she called as Chuck brought the wagon to a halt.

"Good morning, Reba. It's nice to see you this fine morning. Looks like you're already hard at work today."

"Someone has to keep these ledgers in balance, and since I'm being paid to do it, I suppose it should be me. I was just about to head into the office and get a cup of coffee off the stove. Care to join me?"

"I'd love to. Just give me a minute to tie up my horse and I'll be right in." Suddenly remembering his brother sitting beside him in the wagon, Chuck added, "We're actually here to see Mr. Sellers. Any chance he's in the office?"

"No. He went out to the new property to survey the field preparations. He should return in just a bit. Were you aware of that fact that Mr. Sellers purchased a great deal of new acreage? He even hired a new foreman."

"What about Clark? Did he leave?" asked John.

"Oh, Clark is still here. He's in charge of the original acreage. Mr. Sellers just promoted Steven Smith as a second foreman to manage the working of the new fields."

"Steven Smith? He's a good man. Good for him," said John. "Since we have a bit before Mr. Sellers returns, I think I'm going to head over to the bunkhouse and see if anyone's still around to say hello. Want to join me, Chuck?"

"I think I'm going to take Reba up on that offer of coffee. I'll catch up with you later, brother."

As Reba led the way to the office, Chuck said, "I'm sure Clark is fond of the idea of a second foreman." As he made the comment, his voice was dripping with sarcasm.

"Why wouldn't he be? Many hands make light work. He'd be a fool to turn down good help."

"It's not the help Clark will have a problem with. It's the fact that he no longer has sole control of the men. He doesn't like the idea of sharing authority with anyone, nor does he like anyone else having the ear of the big boss. This should be an interesting planting season."

"Chuck, I never thought you'd be so cynical. After the way Mr. Sellers was so gracious to you and John, taking you under his wing and entrusting a piece of land to you, I would have thought you'd be much more gracious and extend people the benefit of the doubt, choosing to believe the best of them. I'm disappointed."

Chuck felt his face go hot. Was he embarrassed? Why should he care what this girl thought of him? She didn't know what went on in the bunkhouse. Just because she could read a ledger book didn't mean she knew anything about working a farm! But the truth was, Chuck did care what Reba thought of him, which is why he replied as he did. "You're right. I should give Clark the benefit of the doubt. He's a good man and I'm sure he and Steven will make this farm the most profitable in the whole region."

Those words were greeted with a smile. Oh. My. Word. Chuck would say whatever he had to say if it meant that he could see that smile just one more time.

"Come on in the office, Chuck. I need to get the coffeepot off the stove and pour us a cup before the whole mess burns. Also, I want you to tell me all about that new farm of yours. I was stunned when Mr. Sellers told me you and John were striking out on your own. I think that's a most excellent decision on your part."

*****

John found a couple of the men near the bunkhouse and tried to strike up a conversation with them. These were men he'd spent thousands of hours working alongside, but you wouldn't know it from the tone of the conversation. "We're so honored you could find the time to come speak with us lowly farmhands. I'm surprised you'd stoop so low as to be seen around the bunkhouse, now that you and Chuck own your own house. Boys, count yourselves fortunate that the Kindig brothers still remember who we are!"

"Jake, what are you talking about? You're just kidding, right?"

"Sure, John, I'm just kidding you." But the look on Jake's face said this was anything but a joke to him. "Sorry I can't stick around to hear all about your new place. Some of us have work to do today. Come on, fellas. Us working stiffs don't have the liberty of shooting the breeze all day."

As the men John thought were his friends walked away, he saw Mr. Sellers and Steven Smith heading toward the office in the wagon. He cut over and met Smith and Sellers as they were tying up the horses. As they climbed the front stairs of the building, they heard laughter. They entered to see Reba and Chuck sitting in the office enjoying their coffee.

"Steven, how good to see you," Chuck said as he grabbed the man and locked him in a strong hug. "Reba was telling me that you're heading up a new crew and are responsible for working Mr. Sellers's new fields. Congratulations! And hello to you, Mr. Sellers. You're looking good this fine morning."

Sellers, John, and Steven looked at each other for a minute, wondering what in the world had happened to Chuck. He'd always been a fun-loving, gregarious guy, but this morning, well, they had to wonder if someone had spiked his coffee with some bootleg whiskey. His cheeks were high in color and his eyes were twinkling.

"Uh, thank you, Chuck. It's good to see you too," said Steven. "What brings you to the farm this morning?"

"Mr. Sellers has been so kind as to offer John and me one of his trusty old plows. We borrowed a wagon from Mr. Fredericks to come over here and pick it up this morning. When you weren't here, Reba offered me a cup of coffee while I waited."

"We won't keep you any longer," said Mr. Sellers. "I had Clark bring the plow up this morning. It's sitting out back. Steven, would you mind helping us load it in the boys' wagon?"

"Be happy to," replied Steven.

"Reba, thank you so much for the coffee and the conversation. If you and your mother would be willing to measure those windows and sew us some curtains, we'd be grateful. We're doing everything we can to make that old shack a home. The possums weren't too happy about their eviction, but the place just wasn't big enough for all of us."

Reba giggled and said, "Mother and I will stop over on Saturday morning, if that works for you. I'm looking forward to seeing your new spread."

After they had loaded the old plow in the wagon, John said, "Mr. Sellers, we can't thank you enough for this. We know we've got hard work ahead of us, but thanks to what we learned from our dad and the experience we gained working for you, we think we're up to the task."

"I have every confidence in you both. Let me know if I can be of further help."

As the brothers started down the road toward their farm, they saw Clark coming in from the fields. "Fancy running into you two over here at our place. What brings you to this neck of the woods?" asked Clark.

"Mr. Sellers gave us this old plow to get us started at our new place. We came to pick it up. How are things with you these days? We heard you've got some new help running the men."

"You heard right, John. Sellers promoted Steven Smith." If the boys thought they'd hear more, they were wrong. Clark didn't seem inclined to add further commentary.

John wasn't satisfied with such a short answer. He wanted to know if sparks were flying in the bunkhouse. "How are you dealing with that, Clark? You've always been the lone second-in-command. Must be quite an adjustment."

"Well, you'd think so, but it's actually been a good addition. I'm not gonna lie. When Sellers first gave you boys control of that cotton field, I had issues with it. Memory serves, I told you I wasn't happy about the situation. It was a blow to my pride, and at first, I was determined to take you two down a notch. But something happened during that growing season. One night when I took some papers to the office, I just exploded and spouted off in frustration to Reba. That girl's a good listener, but she's an even better talker.

"Once I'd finished my rant, she asked me if my problem was with you boys or with Sellers. It was then that I realized I had nothing against you two. I was just mad at Sellers for overlooking me and promoting you. Reba pointed out that Sellers hadn't overlooked me. After all, he was the one who promoted me from hand to foreman all those years ago. Who was I to begrudge you boys the same opportunity I had been afforded? Mr. Sellers is a fair man. If he had enough confidence in you to promote you, I needed to respect his decision—and respect you.

"When I started to feel the familiar sting of resentment hearing of Steven's promotion, I reminded myself of lessons I'd learned earlier. I congratulated Steven on his promotion, and then I got a surprise. Sellers called me into the office and gave me a raise and a promotion! He said he'd been watching the way I handled myself with all that happened with you boys and then the promotion of Steven. He said he appreciated the integrity I'd shown and promoted me to senior foreman! Just goes to show you can't rush things. Once I determined that I would do the job in front of me to the best of my ability and quit worrying about other people's business, things sure worked out."

"I'm glad to hear that things are going well for you. And congratulations on that promotion," Chuck said. "John and I certainly appreciate everything you've done for us over the years, and we wish you all the best. Now I'm sorry to rush off, but we've got to get back to work. Have a good one, Clark."

Once the wagon was down the road a bit, John spoke up. "Never thought I'd hear Clark be so levelheaded about things. He actually seems to be OK with Steven's promotion."

"You heard the story. Sellers promoted him, too."

"That's true. Hey, while we're talking about things that are surprising, I have to tell you about the fellas in the bunkhouse. When you went in to talk to Reba, I went over there to see how the guys were doing. They treated me like I was a skunk, and Jake was the worst of 'em. After all we've been through together over the years, I'd have thought they'd be happy to see one of their own make it out and on to their own land."

"Reminds me of the stories Nehemiah Fisher told us about the way his workers treated him when he took over running the gin. Jealousy is an ugly thing, brother. It takes folks awhile to get used to change, especially when they've been left behind. What I will say I'm struck by, however, is the advice Reba gave to Clark. She's one interesting woman, and I can't figure out how she got to be so smart."

"Why, brother, if I didn't know better, I'd say you're sweet on that girl," John said as he slugged his brother in the arm.

"Am not! I'm just saying she's interesting, is all. And helpful. She and her mother are gonna sew us some curtains. That'll make the old shack feel a little more like a home."

"Wonder why Reba is going out of her way to sew us curtains. Maybe she's a little smitten by you. Though what she'd possibly find attractive about you is a mystery to me." Now it was Chuck's turn to slug his big brother in the arm.

CHAPTER 10

"Dadgum it, Chuck! You'd think a man would be smarter than a mule, but honestly, I'd prefer a mule to you right now!"

"I'm happy to trade places with you, brother, if you think you'd do a better job than me. Because I know for a fact I'd do a better job driving that plow than what you're doing. Remind me, are we plowing lines or circles?"

The boys had been at each other's throats for days now. They were working hard to sow their first field of cotton and it seemed that nothing was going right. They'd decided against buying a mule since it would have meant borrowing money and had opted instead to pull the plow with their own strong backs. Mr. Sellers gave the boys an old seed drill his men no longer used. What should have been a blessing had actually become their nemesis. That stubborn seed drill had given them so many fits, they considered just planting the entire field by hand. After hours of working on the piece of equipment, they'd managed to get it to work. As soon as they plowed these final rows, they'd be ready to plant.

When the boys took a break, Chuck looked out toward the road and saw a car coming their way. As the car drew closer, he could see that it was being driven by Reba with her mother on the bench beside her. "We've got company, John. Reba and her mom are here to check on our window shades."

"Again I will ask, why in the world do we need curtains? I'm not spending a cent on fabric for something we have no need of at this time. If I'm going to part with my hard-earned money, it's going to be to buy a good mule to replace the stubborn one I've got pulling my plow right now!"

"You can stand in this field and run your mouth all you want. I'm going up to the house to greet our guests," Chuck said, and with that, he started toward the house with John grudgingly following behind.

"Miss Reba, how are you this fine morning? And Mrs. Johnson, it is indeed a pleasure to see you. Thank you for accompanying your daughter to our homestead."

"Good morning, Chuck," said Mrs. Johnson. "When Reba told me you and John had bought your own place, I couldn't believe it. This is a nice spread you have here. Your mother must be very proud of you both."

"Thank you, ma'am. Our momma is very proud of what we're doing. She only wishes she was in better health so she could be a help to us getting the house in order. When Miss Reba volunteered your services to help us get this old farmhouse looking like a home, we knew everything would be just fine. We're very grateful for your help. The place definitely could use some work."

Reba spoke up: "Let's go have a look. Mother, shall we?" John and Chuck helped the ladies out of the car and the foursome headed toward the farmhouse.

"I know it's not much to look at right now, but we've come a long way," said John. "Our first order of business was to clear out the family of possums that had taken up residence. They didn't go willingly, but eventually, they did go. We've given the place a good scrubbing. Please forgive us for not having any coffee to offer you ladies; we've been working the fields this morning. We're nearly ready to put our first cotton in the ground."

"We're not here for coffee, John. We're here to measure for curtains," said Mrs. Johnson. "Reba tells me you're interested in curtains and some other touches to make the place more homey. Have you selected fabric? They have some lovely fabrics at the mercantile. And I'm sure we can look through the catalog there to find a few other touches that will make this place look more like a home and less like a . . ."

"Shack," said Chuck, finishing her thought. "Like we said, we know it's not much to look at right now. But it's ours. Welcome, ladies, to our home."

Reba's first impression of the space was that it was awfully small. She'd grown up in town, the daughter of a banker. Her childhood home was very comfortable and had been outfitted with the latest conveniences—electric lights, indoor plumbing, lovely rugs, and comfortable furnishings. Chuck and John's farmhouse consisted of one room. There was a woodstove and basin on one side of the room, two twin beds on the other side of the room, and a large fireplace centered along the back wall with two wooden chairs and a table in front of it. Noticeably absent was a water closet—she supposed the outhouse wasn't too far away. Also absent were electric lights. An oil lamp sat in the middle of the table, and various lanterns and candles were scattered around. After taking it all in, Reba quietly said, "Boys, it's perfect."

"I'm sorry, what was that?" John asked.

"I said, it's perfect. Your home is absolutely perfect."

The look on Mrs. Johnson's face showed that she did not share the opinion of her daughter. "I'm sure there are improvements that can be made. What is your budget, gentlemen?"

"Well, that's still up for debate," said Chuck. "It seems we've sunk all of our money into the purchase of the land and farmhouse, so we don't have much left over for improvements right now. We were just wondering if there was anything that could be done with some of the cotton sacks we have in storage. We just need some towels and maybe a window covering, and when Reba offered to do some sewing for us, we thought maybe she could work with what we have on hand."

Seeing the look on her mother's face, Reba knew the woman was appalled at the thought of linens made of cotton sacks. She quickly jumped in before her mother had a chance to voice her disapproval. "Mother, I'm sure we can do something lovely with the cotton sacks, can't we? John, would you please gather up some of the sacks you'd like for us to use? Mother, I will measure this window and will be right along. I'll meet you at the car. Chuck, could you help me with the measurements?"

John escorted Mrs. Johnson to the barn to retrieve the sacks they had laid aside for linens. Chuck and Reba went to the window to take measurements. "I'm so sorry for my mother's obvious disdain. She's always been used to a certain standard of living and anything less, in her mind, is barbaric. She thinks I'm out of my mind because I want to work for Mr. Sellers on the farm. Mother has no idea what it's like to work, nor does she ever want to find out. She went straight from her father's house to my father's house. She is an excellent hostess at parties and she is very proficient at spending my father's money, but she's never had to work for anything or save money for a purchase. When she wants something, she puts it on Father's account at the mercantile and, magically, the bill gets paid.

"I have tremendous respect for what you and John have done here. You worked hard and you've used your hard-earned money to purchase something for yourselves. You may only own a few acres right now, but I know your work ethic and I've seen your ambition, so I know that this farm is just the beginning for you and John. I'm just so proud that you're doing things the right way. I've seen what happens when people overextend themselves and bite off more than they can chew.

"One night when I was about fourteen years old, a man came to our house late into the evening. I was supposed to be in bed asleep, but the pounding on the door woke me up. I snuck to my bedroom door and opened it just a crack so I could see what was going on. My father was in the foyer of our house speaking with the man who was obviously very distressed. The man was begging, saying if my father wouldn't help him, his life was over. The man was weeping and at one point, he fell to his knees and grabbed my father's pant leg. It was all very disturbing.

"The next morning at the breakfast table, I confessed to my father that the visitor had awoken me and that I had witnessed a good deal of the exchange. I asked my father why the man was so desperate. He explained to me that the man had borrowed money from the bank—more money than he could now repay because of a series of unforeseeable events and poor business decisions—so the bank had no choice but to foreclose on the loan. The man and his family were being evicted from their house and had nowhere to go.

"I was shocked. I told my father I could not believe he would kick a family out of their house! My father smiled at me and told me he loved my sense of compassion, but then proceeded to explain to me the nature of borrowing money. I will never forget what he said—it has stuck with me to this day. He said that the Bible is exactly right when it says that the borrower is always slave to the lender. He said that people do not understand that when they borrow money, they must be smart about it, because they are indenturing themselves to a master until they can pay that money back. This man spent his income like it was his to spend. He didn't understand that until he repaid his loan, his money was not really his own—it belonged to the bank. His choices were now not only affecting him but also his whole family. The man had children who now would be homeless!

"After that conversation at the breakfast table, I determined that I would learn all I could about managing money. I know my mother has big plans for me to marry well and live the good life just like she has, but I want to gain wisdom and understanding so that whether I have a husband who can take care of me or if I am left to make my own way in the world, I will be just fine. Money is a very useful tool when it is in the hands of someone who knows how to use it. Money in the hands of a fool leads to heartache, which is what that man and his family came to know firsthand."

Chuck didn't know what to say. He'd never thought much about money, because he'd never had any money to think about, but what Reba was saying made sense. He and John had decided not to borrow any money to buy their piece of land, even though they'd been given the opportunity to do so and could have bought much more acreage if they had. Solomon, the head of the cotton exchange, had told the brothers he would be willing to lend them money against the value of their cotton. The man who had sold them the farm told the boys he knew of a local banker who would lend them some money against the value of their land. They'd kicked around the idea of contacting that banker to get a loan so they could buy a brand-new plow and a mule or two. When Chuck was hitched to that plow and getting yelled at by his brother, he had a tendency to second-guess their decision not to borrow, but hearing the story Reba just told confirmed in his mind that they'd done the right thing. There would be plenty of time and money to buy a mule or two once they'd harvested another good crop. Until then, they'd make do with what they had and sleep well at night knowing they were slaves to no one.

"Reba, you are the prettiest and smartest woman I've ever known. Would it be OK if I called on you next Saturday night?"

"My goodness, Chuck, I wish you'd stop beating around the bush and just say what you're thinking," Reba teased. Chuck blushed. He couldn't believe he'd come right out and asked if he could call on her! She must think him an idiot.

Seeing Chuck's embarrassment, Reba quickly said, "I'd be delighted if you'd come to call Saturday evening. Of course, you know you'll have to visit with my father before he'll let you across the threshold. But I assure you've met him before, so you know he's harmless."

"Saturday night it is, then."

With the cotton sacks loaded into the car, Reba and Mrs. Johnson drove away, and the brothers returned to the field. Working until they could no longer see to run the seed drill in the darkness, they managed to get the cotton seeds in the ground. Now they would remember the words of Solomon and do just as he said—work like it all depended on them, and pray like it all depended on God.

CHAPTER 11

C huck took one last look at his reflection in the window as he waited for someone to answer his knock at the door. He'd never called on a lady before, and especially not one of Reba's caliber. His mouth felt like it was full of sawdust and his stomach felt like it could betray him at any time and vomit up the beans he'd had for lunch.

Just as he was considering running from the front porch and heading back to the farm, the door opened, and before him stood Mr. Johnson. The man could buy and sell Chuck many times over. He was so successful and respected in town, and Chuck was just a lowly dirt farmer. "Good evening, Chuck. Reba told me you'd be coming to call. How can I help you this evening?"

Say something, you idiot! "Um, yes. Good evening, Mr. Johnson. Um, yes. Would Reba be available, or, I mean would you do me the honor . . . ? Could Reba accompany me on a walk this evening?"

"I'm quite certain she's capable of taking a stroll, son. Let me see if she's interested in doing it. Please come in while I fetch her."

Chuck stepped into the foyer and immediately wanted to turn and leave. The Johnson's foyer was nearly half the size of his entire house. He was way out of his league here. He was a fool to think this girl would possibly see anything attractive in him—or his offer to go for a walk. This girl was obviously used to the finer things in life, and he'd bummed a ride into town from his neighbor because he didn't even own a mule. But then Reba entered the foyer and every thought left his head.

"Good evening, Chuck. I must say, you clean up very well. I don't know that I've ever seen you outside of the farm."

"I took a bath this afternoon." Had he really just said that—*I took a bath*? If there had been any question before, Chuck had just confirmed that he was, indeed, the village idiot.

Reba's lilting laugh filled the foyer, and made Chuck lower his head and blush. When Chuck lifted his head and looked at Mr. Johnson, he saw the most amazing thing. The man was smiling. He'd been certain Mr. Johnson would never allow his daughter to leave the house with a rube like him, but there the man was, smiling. "You kids enjoy your stroll. Reba, Mother and I will lay out some lemonade and cookies for you and Chuck to enjoy on the front porch when you return. You'd best be on your way, the sun will be setting in a bit."

Chuck held out his arm and Reba took it. A whole parade of elephants could have been tromping through the town square, and Chuck wouldn't have noticed. He only had eyes for the girl on his arm. He and Reba talked of farming and Mr. Sellers and the weather and just about everything else under the sun. At the end of their time together, Chuck felt refreshed and was already planning another opportunity to spend time with Reba.

He thanked Mr. and Mrs. Johnson for the opportunity to call on Reba and thanked them for their hospitality. As he walked back toward the edge of town where his ride was waiting to take him back to the farm, he couldn't help but feel that if a girl like Reba could care about him, there was nothing too difficult for him to accomplish.

*****

"Brother, I can't believe it, but we've harvested another bumper crop of cotton! I've checked and rechecked our numbers, and they are stellar. Once we get this crop to the gin, we'll decide how much seed to keep for next year and how much we'll sell. Thankfully, Mr. Sellers is going to let us ride in with him to visit Solomon at the cotton exchange. I wonder what the crops are selling for this season. Surely it's going to be even higher than what we got last year. I think we just may be able to do this farming thing!"

Chuck barely heard a word his brother was saying. Yes, he was happy with the harvest, but he'd found himself thinking more and more about matters outside of his work. He thought about Reba. The more time he spent with her, the more time he wanted to spend with her. He also enjoyed his conversations with Mr. Johnson. The man challenged his old ways of thinking. For the first time in his life, Chuck considered the world outside the farm and dared to believe he might have a place in it.

Mr. Johnson seemed to have a grasp of just about everything. He engaged Chuck in discussions about his farm, the status of the crops, and about Chuck's family. He had given Chuck solid advice on financial matters, business, relationships, even on his walk with God. He was brilliant and confident and successful and respected in the community, and obviously quite a capable provider for his family. The more he knew of Mr. Johnson, the more he wanted to emulate him. By his words and example, the man made Chuck think bigger, inspiring him to continue his quest for knowledge and understanding.

Though the voice deep inside Chuck grew louder and more insistent, telling him there might be more to God's plan for his life than farming, he knew there was no way he could explain that to his brother. For John, it was cut and dried. They were farmers. Always had been, always would be. John saw his road to success consisting of nothing more than the pursuit to own more land, the effort to farm that land, and the determination to make a healthy profit off the sale of each harvest. Each year looked the same as the last. At one time, Chuck may have been satisfied with that, but now he wanted more. The next chance he had, Chuck decided he would talk with Mr. Johnson about this yearning he was feeling. The man knew everything else; surely he could help Chuck sort through his thoughts on this issue.

CHAPTER 12

"Chuck, did you hear what I said? Are you in agreement that we need to buy a mule with the first dollars we bring in from selling this cottonseed?"

"Yes, John, of course we need a mule. That makes sense." The brothers were on their way home from the cotton gin, and Chuck was beyond distracted. He'd gone over a million different scenarios in his head, trying to figure out the best way to tell his brother about the restlessness he'd been feeling.

Chuck was pulled from his thoughts by an elbow to his ribs. "I asked if you were expecting company. Whose car is that in front of our house?" John asked. Chuck didn't recognize the automobile. To the best of his knowledge, they weren't expecting any visitors that day.

As the boys walked up to the house, a man they had never seen before emerged from the car. "Good afternoon, gentlemen. Are you the owners of this property?"

"Yes, sir. We are. And who might you be?" asked John.

"My name is Tom Brown. I'm a member of the Southwestern Association of Petroleum Geologists, and if you have a moment, I'd like to talk to you about your farm."

"Come on inside," said Chuck. "I don't know what we can tell you that would interest . . . what did you call yourself? A petroleum geologist? I don't even know that that is, so I certainly don't know how I can help you, but you're welcome to come inside."

Once the men had settled inside, Tom Brown began to speak. "Petroleum geologists are scientists who study the earth to determine where oil might be located under the surface. Have you gentlemen been keeping up with some of the news out of Oklahoma City about recent oil discoveries?"

"Can't say that we have. We've stayed pretty busy here, getting our farm up and running," said John. "What's been happening up in Oklahoma City?"

"Well," Tom continued, "it used to be that the primary way to know if oil was underneath the surface of the earth was to look for evidences of the oil seeping up out of the ground. This is called 'creekology,' because so often, the oil would show up on the surface of a creek—hence the name, creekology. Sometimes, people would stumble across oil when they'd be drilling water wells, but mostly, creekology was the means of oil discovery. Until lately. Scientists like myself have found a way to determine if there's oil under the ground without seeing evidence of it on the surface. Gentlemen, my colleagues and I have every reason to believe that your farm is sitting on top of an oil field. We'd like to do some exploration to see if our assumption is correct."

The brothers sat there staring at their guest, unsure of what to say. Seeing the glazed look in the eyes of his hosts, Tom spoke up, "You will, of course, be paid by the oil company for giving them the right to drill on your land, and, if oil is discovered, you will be entitled to royalties. I've brought along some paperwork for you to review. It lists our reasons for believing there is oil under your farm and it outlines your initial rights during the drilling process. I can leave the documents with you to review and set a time to come back to answer any additional questions you may have. I can also put you in contact with representatives from the oil company who will be doing the drilling, should you consent to allow them to do so. Would that be acceptable?"

"Yes. That would be acceptable. Please do leave your papers. My brother and I will have to discuss the matter, of course," said John.

"Here you are. I've included a card with my name and phone number on it, as well as the name and phone number of a representative at the oil company. Please take your time and call me with any questions you may have. I look forward to visiting with you again soon. And, gentlemen, if what we believe is true, let me congratulate you. This is the kind of thing that can change a life."

The brothers saw their guest to the door. As they watched him drive away, not one word was spoken. Oil? Under their farm?

John broke the silence. "Brother, we are in way over our heads here."

"I know exactly who we can ask for guidance. Come on, John, let's go to town."

*****

"Mr. Johnson, please. I don't have an appointment, but if you'll tell him Chuck is here and needs a word, I'm hoping he'll see me." As soon as the geologist left the farm, having dropped his bombshell on the brothers, Chuck and John headed to town to get some advice. Surely Mr. Johnson would be able to point them in the right direction, or at least tell them if this was a scam or if the news of oil under their farm was legitimate.

"Chuck. John. What brings you to town this late in the day?"

"Mr. Johnson, thank you for allowing us to barge in on you like this. If you have a minute, my brother and I have something very important that we'd like to run by you," Chuck said.

"Of course boys, come on back." As Mr. Johnson ushered the brothers into his office, John spoke first.

"Mr. Johnson, this afternoon we were paid a visit by a man who said he was part of a group of geologists somewhere up near Oklahoma City. He said this group believed there is oil under our farm and then he left us this big bundle of papers to read. Neither Chuck nor I can even begin to know what we should be looking for in all those words. We were hoping that you, being a businessman and all, might be able to look over these and tell us if this is all a scam. We are proud of our farm and know that the soil can sure produce some nice cotton, but it just seems a bit far-fetched to think that there'd be any oil under our tiny patch of land." John handed over the bundle of papers they'd been left.

As Mr. Johnson took his time reading over the documents, Chuck and John studied the floor, looked at the pictures hanging on the wall and looked out the window onto the town square. Just when it seemed Mr. Johnson intended to read all night, he looked up from the stack of papers. "Boys, I don't want to overstate anything and get your hopes up, but this paperwork looks legitimate to me. I've heard of this association of petroleum geologists and I know what they've been doing up around the Oklahoma City area. These men are for-ward-thinkers and, from what I've read and heard, they're great sci-entists. If they believe there is oil under your farm—enough to send one of their own out here to speak with you—then there probably is oil under your farm. And, gentlemen, if there is, you need to be prepared for what's coming."

"What do you mean by that? What's coming? Are they going to tear up our land so we can't plant crops this coming season? Because that's just not acceptable," John said.

"John, having them tear up your land is the least of your con-cerns. If there is oil under your land, you're not going to have to worry about planting crops. Oil revenues will pay your bills. If you are able to negotiate a fair contract for drilling on your land and payment of royalties in perpetuity, well, this could change your lives. You wanted to make a better future for your family, this will do it.

"Before I say any more, I want to have one of my attorney friends look over this paperwork. Boys, do you mind if I hold on to this for a few days and then get back to you?"

The brothers didn't know what to say, so they simply nodded in assent.

"Excellent. Give me a few days to get some firm answers for you boys and then we'll get together and talk. And, boys, I would advise you against sharing this information with too many people just yet. Once word of this gets out, there will be people coming out of the woodwork asking for a moment of your time. Some of these people will have your best interests at heart, but others most definitely will not. I trust a word to the wise is sufficient."

*****

The next morning dawned, and Chuck awoke to find John already up and drinking coffee on the front porch. He poured himself a cup and joined his brother.

"I couldn't sleep. I just kept thinking about what that geologist fellow said and what Mr. Johnson told us. How many days do you think it will take him to get back to us? We need to have an answer to give to that fellow. If there's really money under our dirt, that changes everything. No more scratching to get by. No more living hand to mouth. We're going places, brother. If only Dad could see us now." John's eyes got ever wider as he spoke. Chuck almost thought he could see dollar signs in them.

"Hey, I forgot to mention, but I'm going to church with Reba and her family today. After church, I'm going to their house for lunch and then we're attending an ice cream social this evening. I probably won't be back till after sundown."

"Why do you have to pick today to start going to church? We have so much we need to talk over. Not just about this news from the geologist but also about what we're going to do with the money from our latest crop. We have to decide on a mule. There's no time to waste on ice cream socials and walks in the park with your girl. Where are your priorities, brother?"

"John, I trust you to find a mule, if you think that's what we need. This is just something that I promised Reba I'd do with her. I'll be back this evening, and tomorrow, we can take care of some of those things on your to-do list, if you want. Now, I've got to get cleaned up and head into town. I'll see you tonight."

CHAPTER 13

"Gentlemen, I've had the chance to visit with a few of my colleagues, and I think I have some answers for you." Chuck and John were sitting across the desk from Mr. Johnson in his office at the bank. "First of all, this offer is real and there is a legitimate possibility that the oil reserves currently sitting underground at your farm may be substantial. I took the liberty of contacting the geological association and the drilling company to make further inquiries, representing myself as your financial advisor. This is the kind of money that will change your lives and the lives of your descendants for many generations to come, if handled correctly."

"What do you mean by that, 'if handled correctly'?" John asked.

"I would recommend that you enlist the assistance of someone familiar with finance to have them guide you in the best places to deposit your money to get the best returns. Money can work for you, if you place it in the right hands and don't just spend willy-nilly."

"Couldn't you advise us, Mr. Johnson?" asked Chuck.

"I know how to run a savings and loan, but I don't have the kind of experience necessary to advise you on financial planning. I would recommend you consult with someone who specializes in this field. I have a colleague in Oklahoma City who would do a good job for you. He's a man of integrity and great vision. I can arrange a meeting, if you'd like."

"Please do," said Chuck. "I'd like to know just what kind of money we're talking about, and the sooner, the better."

The brothers left and started the walk toward home. John was the first to speak: "No more walking for us, brother. As soon as some of that oil money comes in, we're buying a car. And we'll definitely expand the acreage we own. I've heard about some farms coming up for sale. I'll make some inquiries. Can you believe our good fortune?"

"John, it seems like you're spending this new fortune before we've seen a single penny of it! We've got to slow down and be smart about this. We come from dirt farmers and don't know the first thing about handling money. Don't you think we need to talk to someone before we do anything else?"

"I don't see anything wrong with making a few plans on our own. We may come from dirt farmers, but we've got as much sense as anyone else! It seems like these days, you put more trust in the Johnsons than you do your own flesh and blood!"

After John said those words, Chuck thought it best to walk the rest of the way back to the farm in silence. What had happened to his brother? He'd always been the voice of reason who'd kept Chuck from running headlong into harebrained schemes. Now it seemed like the two brothers had changed places. Had John forgotten what their quest was all about in the first place? Did he think that just because they had some money in the bank and some successes, that they didn't need to continue seeking for wisdom and knowledge?

When Chuck thought back on all he'd learned so far, it only made him realize how much more he still had to learn. He owed so much to the men who had already built into his life. He thought about Mr. Sellers. When he and John first thought of asking Mr. Sellers to share knowledge about what it takes to gain wealth and success, they believed there wasn't much of a chance the man would agree to do so. To their surprise, not only did he agree to share his wisdom and knowledge with them, he'd given of his profits and equipment to help them get started farming their own land—the first members of their family ever to do so. Were it not for Mr. Sellers, who knew where Chuck might be right now.

He thought about Nehemiah Fisher, the owner of the cotton gin. Nehemiah said he got where he was today by paying careful attention to the business around him and looking for every opportunity to advance. He said if you showed yourself to be trustworthy, good things would happen. Isn't that what had happened for him and John? They'd paid careful attention to all Mr. Sellers taught them, and then when the opportunity presented itself, they moved out into new and greater things.

He also thought about the words Nehemiah shared concerning persevering through adversity. How they'd come to understand the importance of that lesson! When their fellow farmhands had tried to sabotage their efforts with that first cotton crop, he and John had pressed on and won the respect of their peers. When they moved off the Sellers farm and onto their own land, the tongues were certainly wagging then. Everyone was betting against the Kindig boys' ability to make it on their own, but they'd proven the naysayers wrong. This discovery of oil on their land was sure to bring with it a whole new crop of trouble, but Chuck was determined nothing would deter him from continuing his quest.

In that way, he was like Solomon at the cotton exchange. Solomon, though he was already a very successful man in his own right, stressed the importance of continuing the search for wisdom and knowledge. If Solomon thought there were still things he needed to learn, how much more should Chuck have that same attitude? Again he thought of the words of Solomon: "When it comes to business, work like it all depends on you and pray like it all depends on God." Maybe this restlessness he'd been feeling in his spirit was an indication that it was time to do some praying to see what God would have him do next.

Chuck thought of Joseph Hillman. Now that was an impressive man! He wasn't sure what the definition of "self-made man" exactly was, but he was pretty sure Joseph would qualify as a self-made man. Just like John and himself, Joseph had come from nothing. Now he was a respected and influential businessman. More than any other lessons Joseph shared with the brothers, the ones that stood out in Chuck's mind were the principles of saving and giving. Joseph taught the boys that it was important for them to save back some of their crop so they'd have something to sow later. He also taught them that it was important to give away a portion of what you have to make sure your possessions don't get control of you. Following the principles Joseph Hillman had laid out had given the brothers a sense of peace, because no matter what, they knew their financial house was in order. All indications were this oil would bring a windfall into the Kindig coffers. They'd have to be more careful than ever to ensure that the influx of money didn't get control of their hearts and minds.

As they arrived home and prepared for bed in silence, Chuck couldn't help but wonder if John remembered all the lessons they'd learned as clearly as he did. His words and actions seemed to indicate that he did not. Maybe this financial advisor in Oklahoma City could talk some sense into John and get him back on the right path. Chuck certainly knew he could not wait to hear what he had to say.

CHAPTER 14

John and Chuck walked into the offices of Mr. David Mills promptly at 10:00 a.m. The relationship between the brothers had been strained since that walk home from Mr. Johnson's office a week earlier. Chuck was hoping that what they would learn today from Mr. Mills would go a long way toward easing that tension and bring peace back into their home again.

Mr. Mills was young—much younger than either brother expected him to be—but when he began to speak, it was obvious that he was wise beyond his years. "John, Chuck, thank you for coming all this way to visit with me. Mr. Johnson has filled me in on your circumstances, and I must say, I found them amazing. It would be my pleasure to help you establish a financial plan that will benefit you and yours for years to come. First of all, let me hear from you. What are some of your goals for your money?"

Neither of the brothers had ever heard such a question: What are your goals for your money? Money had been scarce all their lives, so their only goal to date was that their money would stretch to cover all their expenses. John was the first to speak. "I would like to buy a car. And some more land. And I'd like to build a bigger house with more than one room and with running water and indoor plumbing."

"Those are fair ambitions," David said. "Chuck, what about you? What are your goals for your money?"

"Well," Chuck began, "I agree with my brother. It would be nice to have more than one room to live in. And having our own car would be nice. We had to borrow a truck from Mr. Sellers to drive up here today. But mostly, I want to make sure that we do everything we can to ensure that we and our entire family are never hard up for money again. Is there a way to do that, Mr. Mills? Is there a plan that will take care of both what we need today and what we need and want tomorrow? We've had some wise people give us advice and it seems like all of them say it is important to plan for tomorrow and not eat all your seed today."

"I'm glad you asked, Chuck. Yes, there is a way to manage your money so it works for you and your family well into the future. And I also think we can find a little something to get you a car and maybe add on a room or two to your house."

David Mills began showing John and Chuck a suggested investment plan. Though the concepts were mostly foreign to the brothers, David explained them in such a way that they understood exactly how the plan would work. Chuck, especially, was intrigued with the idea of investing and letting your money do the work for you.

"I think I understand what you've laid out here and I'm fully in favor of all of it," said Chuck. "I just have one more question—and this is pretty important to me. I want to give away a portion of all the money that flows into our account. Someone once told us that's a good thing to do. Do you have any suggestions about where or how we could give some of our money away? I want to make sure it goes to a place that can help people who may be down on their luck."

"You are a wise man, Chuck. I think I know just the place. It's actually located right here in Oklahoma City, and I can see if they can get you in for a visit today, if you'd like to take a look around to see what your money would be helping. Would you like for me to make a call and arrange that visit?"

Chuck looked at his brother, waiting for his reply. "Yes, I think that would be a good idea," said John. "Please do make that call."

*****

The John 3:16 Mission sat in a depressed part of Oklahoma City. As the car pulled into the lot, Chuck saw a group of men gathered around a small table by the front door, playing cards. The brothers got out of the car and went inside and were greeted by a young man wearing an apron.

"Welcome, friends! My name is Joshua. How can I be of service to you today?"

"My name is John Kindig. This is my brother, Chuck. I believe David Mills called to tell you we'd be stopping in."

"Oh, yes! We've been expecting you and are so grateful you've chosen to come and see what we do to help our friends in need. Please, come this way and I'll show you around. Perhaps you'll even choose to help us with this afternoon's meal service, just to get a real feel for the work we do here. Right this way." Joshua led them into a kitchen bustling with workers. The stoves were already hot and good smells were coming from pots scattered across the cooktops. After introducing the brothers to the kitchen manager, Joshua led John and Chuck to a room filled with cots. As they passed through the room, Chuck tried to count the number of cots but lost track. Did this many people truly need a place to sleep each night?

"Chuck, John, why do you want to help us?"

Chuck was startled by the question. It seemed shallow to say, *Well, we've got some money we want to give away and couldn't think of any other place to give it,* so he just replied, "Mr. Mills told us about your work and we wanted to help."

As Chuck turned his attention from all of the cots to Joshua, he noticed that Joshua was looking right at him, but his gaze seemed to go beyond just "looking" at him. It was like Joshua's eyes saw deeper than that and they were filled with such compassion, it was almost overwhelming. Chuck had to look away. He felt like if he looked into the man's eyes for too long, Joshua might see things Chuck didn't want to share right then.

"I'm surely grateful you've come our way. We have plenty of volunteers who are so gracious with their time and talents, but we are desperately in need of those who are willing to give of their means to help our friends."

"I notice you keep calling them 'friends,'" said John. "Maybe I'm confused, but I thought these were just strangers off the streets who had fallen on hard times and need some temporary help getting by. I don't understand your use of the word 'friends' when you refer to them."

"That's a fair question, John. It is true, the people who come to us are in need of temporary assistance. They come here looking for a hot meal or a bed for the night, and we make every effort, with the means at our disposal, to provide for those needs. But if that's all we provide for them, we do them a great disservice. We owe it to them to be their friend. Please indulge me as I try to help you see more clearly. What do you gentlemen do for a living?"

Though he could not see what that question had to do with the question at hand, John answered, "I'm a farmer."

"Ah, I guessed right. I could see the calluses on your hands and the glow on your face brought on by days in the sun. Excellent. Let me ask you, what's more harmful to your crop—an exterior threat like pests or drought, or disease at the plant's root?"

"Definitely a root problem. Pests we can kill. Lack of water, we can fix with irrigation. But if the roots are bad, the plant doesn't stand a chance."

"If you choose to visit with the friends who will come to us today, I want you to notice something. We will give them a hot meal. For those with no place to lay their heads, we will provide them with a safe, warm place to sleep tonight. And yet, you will see that many of our friends still look forlorn. Truth be told, if you look deep into the eyes of those friends who will sit at our tables and partake of our meals and then go to have dinner at the finest steakhouse in this city and look into the eyes of the patrons dining alongside you there, you may notice that the eyes are the same, no matter whether you've begged for your meal or paid full price. Loneliness, despair, hopeless-ness, lack of peace—they hit everyone, regardless of their station in life. That's the disease that eats at the root of all men. We cannot, in good conscience, simply feed these people a hot meal and give them a place to lay their head but then leave them dying in their disease. We must hold out hope to them. That's what a friend would do. Does that make sense?"

John answered, "Joshua, I've lived all my life dirt poor. I find it hard to believe that someone with the means to buy a fine dinner would be as hopeless as the men who will come through your doors. Money has a way of bringing hope."

Joshua smiled kindly, with his eyes as much as with his mouth. "I'm very thankful you're here with us today, John. What I'd ask both of you to do is simply help the men find a place to sit at the tables once they have their food and then help clean up the tables once a group leaves, before the next group comes in to be seated. Being in the midst of our friends will give you the best answer for why we do what we do. If you'll check in with me after the lunch crowd leaves, I'd love to visit with you some more to get your impressions."

Once the doors opened for lunch to be served, it seemed the flow of humanity would never cease. Chuck and John couldn't believe there were that many men who needed help finding food to eat for the day. After two hours on his feet, Chuck paused and sat down in an empty chair across from a man who was eating alone. The man had on what looked to have once been a fairly decent overcoat. His hair didn't look like it had been combed in a good bit, and Chuck couldn't see if his face had been washed because the man refused to look up from his bowl, not even when Chuck tried to strike up a conversation. "Hello there. Beautiful day today, isn't it?" The man hovered over his soup bowl protectively, like an animal, and kept slurping.

"Glad you could join us today," Chuck added. That comment prompted the man to look up from his bowl just long enough for Chuck to see his eyes. There was a hollowness to his gaze, as if anything good and right that had ever existed had been drained from his body. "My name is Chuck. What's your name?"

The man looked up again and studied Chuck's face. Just as Chuck was starting to get uncomfortable, the man replied, "Bill. My name is Bill." Then he lowered his head and went back to his soup.

"Nice to meet you, Bill. Come here often?" What kind of question was that to ask a man eating at a soup kitchen? Chuck was kicking himself for being so stupid.

To his surprise, Bill replied, "I come here a few times a week. Don't want to overstay my welcome."

"Well, I'm proud to make your acquaintance, Bill. Is there anything I can get for you?"

"No, thank you, sir. Thank you for the soup."

Chuck wanted to weep for Bill. What had happened in his life to bring him to this point? Chuck had known lack in his life, but he'd never had to beg for food. He'd never looked in the mirror and seen eyes so devoid of hope staring back at him. No matter what hardship had come his way, he'd always held on to hope. What happens in a life to steal hope from a person?

After the lunch crowd had dissipated, John and Chuck found Joshua to continue their visit. "Gentlemen, how was lunch service?"

John answered, "I can certainly see why you'd need donations. It's hard to believe this many people don't have enough money for their daily bread."

"Did you have a chance to visit with any of our friends?" Joshua asked.

"As a matter of fact, I did," said Chuck. "I sat down opposite a man named Bill. We didn't have much of a conversation because he wouldn't really look up at me, but what I did notice is that Bill seems to have been through something horrible. Joshua, he looked like he has no hope. How does that happen?"

"People lose hope for a variety of reasons: disappointment, pain, loss, just to name a few; but ultimately, they lose hope because they put their hope in the wrong place to start out with. There's a verse in the Bible that might help you understand. Psalm 20:7 says, 'Some trust in chariots, and some in horses: but we will remember the name of the Lord our God.' The friends who come through our doors may have lost jobs, fortunes, houses, even family, and those things may not ever come back to them, but there is One who will never leave them—God. He is always there, just waiting for them to acknowledge his presence so that he can walk beside them and give them hope again. True and lasting hope can't be found anywhere but in God. Everything else is as uncertain as shifting sand. Sharing this truth is the single best thing we can do for our friends. That's why I show up here every day. Soup will fill a stomach and a bed can provide temporary rest, but I'm here to offer the one thing that will provide eternal nourishment and rest. I hold out the Source of hope to our friends."

That night on the ride home, Chuck was lost in thought about everything he'd seen and heard at the mission. He choked back tears as he thought about Bill. As long as he lived, he'd never forget the look in that man's eyes. Nor would he ever forget the message Joshua shared with him that day. He'd been on a quest for wisdom and knowledge so he could change his station in life. He'd thought that owning land and amassing income was what the quest was all about, but was that actually just "trusting in chariots and horses"?

"Chuck, I enjoyed our time in the city today. I guess I've been a little distant lately. I suppose the thought of all this money is overwhelming me. I'm not sure what I think of the mission, of all those men who look so lost, but if you think that giving to that place is the right thing to do, I suppose I could go along with it for a while."

"It's good to have you back, brother. I don't like all that silence in our house. If we can't muster the noise to fill one room, what are we going to do when we build on a few more rooms?"

John laughed at that and continued smiling as the brothers made their way down the road toward home.

CHAPTER 15

"Chuck, are you paying attention? If we want to purchase the Olsen farm, we're going to have to move quickly. Then I propose we put tenant farmers on the land to work it for us. Imagine that—the sons of a tenant farmer are now going to be the landowners! Once we can see our way to it, we'll move to buy another farm. The more land we have, the more money it generates, the more land we can buy. I like this cycle! So are we agreed that we'll go speak with Mr. Olsen tomorrow?"

"Yes," said Chuck. "Er, I mean, no. I can't go tomorrow. I'm headed to Oklahoma City tomorrow."

"When are you going to give that up? You're a landowner now who has responsibilities. You don't have time to play in the stock market and hang around with your friends at the mission, engaging in all that do-gooder stuff. Consider the fact that you employ a growing number of tenant farmers good deed enough."

The geologists had been correct. The drilling company didn't have to sink their equipment too far into the earth to hit the oil that had been hiding underneath the boys' farm. The boys thought they'd made good money off their cotton crops, but what they were making off this oil beat farming a thousand acres of cotton.

Since they could no longer farm on their original land, the boys were looking to purchase other properties using their new wealth. Actually, John was looking to purchase other properties; Chuck's mind was elsewhere. Chuck had been making regular trips to Oklahoma City to visit with David Mills to learn more about investing. After discussing a few trades, David told Chuck he seemed to have a natural mind for investing. Chuck enjoyed reading about companies and had no problem going against common wisdom to pick stocks he felt were undervalued. Though he'd been right so far, he was cautious. He only invested money that was left over after he put back some for the future. Always at the front of his mind was his determination to never go back to the hard-scrabble life from which he'd come. When he was in the city, Chuck also continued to check in at the John 3:16 Mission and was finding himself increasingly drawn to the place.

"John, I made these appointments in the city. I've got to keep my appointments."

"Fine, then I'll go alone to visit with Mr. Olsen. I can negotiate a good deal with or without you."

*****

After his visit with David Mills, Chuck had gone to the mission and was now wiping off tables in the dining room, as there were only a few people still eating toward the end of lunch service. In the back corner, he recognized a familiar face. "Bill, it's good to see you here again today. How are things going?" Bill looked up from his bowl and nodded to acknowledge Chuck's presence.

"You know, with all the faces that come in and out of here, it's kind of good to see a familiar face. I've come to consider you a friend. Would you mind, since there's not many people left in here, if you and I prayed together? I'd like to thank God for bringing you into my life. Also, I've got a lot on my mind and I'd really appreciate having someone join me in praying about it. Would that be OK?" Bill looked up from his bowl and though the nod was almost imperceptible, he gave his assent.

"Wonderful. I really appreciate this, Bill. Let's pray. Father God, I thank you for my friend Bill. I thank you for bringing our lives together. I can tell that Bill is a good man. He is obviously a man of deep thought and wisdom. Thank you for bringing someone like that into my life for this time. God, you know I'm going through a time of great decision. Please show me the right path to walk. Grant me wisdom to make right choices and then courage to follow through on those choices. I thank you in advance for all you're going to do in my life and in Bill's life. In your Son's name we pray, amen."

When Chuck lifted his head, his eyes met Bill's. Chuck could swear he saw a small fire burning behind the tears. "Thank you, Chuck. You have no idea what that meant to me," Bill said.

"Well, thank you, Bill, for praying with me. Sometimes it's just good to have someone praying alongside you when your burdens get heavy. Is there something I can be praying about for you, Bill?"

Bill hesitated and then began to speak. "I haven't always been like this. Down on my luck. In fact, not too terribly long ago, I had a good deal of money to my name. I lived in a nice house with my wife and daughters and thought I had the world by the tail. I was a respected businessman, until one day, one of my business partners didn't show up to work. I thought it was strange that he just wouldn't show up but didn't really start to worry until the same thing happened the next day. And then some officers from the revenue office showed up at my door. It turns out my business partner, the one I'd trusted to handle our finances, was a crook. He'd left town with every penny we had, leaving me holding the bag. He'd neglected to pay our bills. He'd scammed many of our customers out of their life savings.

"I was so angry and ashamed of what my partner had done— using my name, no less. I went home and told my wife everything that had happened. When she found out the trouble I was in, she couldn't handle it. She packed up our daughters and went back to Missouri to live with her parents.

"I was alone and penniless. With nowhere to turn, I started visiting the mission. I just wanted to be invisible and had managed to hide in the crowd, until you came along. It seemed like I couldn't escape you. Every time I came here, you'd be here wiping down tables and you always had a smile for me. Tonight, when you prayed and called me 'a good man' and a man of 'deep thought and wisdom,' . . . Chuck, you have no idea what that meant to me. It was like for the first time in a long time, I had hope that maybe God could see me that way. Your words gave me hope."

*****

Chuck found Joshua doing inventory in the pantry. "I'm going to head home now," Chuck said. "I'll stop in the next time I come to the city."

"Chuck, if you have a minute, I'd like to visit with you. Please come to my office and we can talk."

Joshua's office was not much more than a closet. There was a small desk in the corner with papers scattered all over it. One chair sat in front of the desk. Chuck took that chair as Joshua settled in behind the desk. "Chuck, I can't thank you enough for your consistent efforts and the financial support you and John have given to the mission. Your generosity has made the difference in countless lives."

"That's kind of you to say, Joshua. I certainly enjoy the time I spend here serving others and I believe so strongly in what you do here, I only wish I could give more."

"Funny you should mention that. That's what I wanted to talk to you about. Chuck, I'd like for you and John to serve on the board of directors for the mission. Before you think I'm doing this to thank you for all the money you and John have given, you should know that I have a motive for offering you this position. In order for our mission to grow and be able to serve all those God would bring our way, we will need men of influence to champion our cause and work alongside me to set a course for the future. As I've told you from the first day we met, we do not exist simply to fill the stomachs of the friends who walk through our doors. We exist to hold out the Bread of Life to those God would bring our way. Once they eat that Bread, they will never hunger again but will be empowered to change their lives and the lives of those they come in contact with. If we can positively impact those in our sphere of influence—those God brings through our doors—and then they impact those in their sphere of influence, I'm just a fool enough to believe that could change the world. Are you willing to stand beside me in this pursuit? I know it will mean giving up a great deal of your time, but I'm hoping you'll feel the sacrifice is worth it."

If Joshua had asked this question two years ago, Chuck would have immediately accepted. But now, the stakes were much higher. John was so set on expanding their land holdings, and owning land meant spending time supervising the tending of that land. If John got upset over Chuck's occasional trips to the city, what would he say to this proposal to get even more involved at the mission?

He could always offer to sell his share of the land to John and just hang on to his mineral rights. The oil that was coming out of the ground would give Chuck more than enough money to live on, plus his initial investments were giving him a little extra money on top. But would it be fair to John for him to back out on their partnership?

Then there was Reba. He wasn't sure where that relationship was going, but he knew he wanted it to continue to progress. Would it stall out if he spent the majority of his time in the city? What if it went as far as marriage? Would she be willing to leave her family and move to Oklahoma City?

He and John had come so far on their quest. It was hard to believe that just a short time ago, they were living in a bunkhouse with a bunch of smelly men with no prospect for advancement. Was this the next step in the quest; was this God's plan for him? He just wasn't sure.

"Joshua, I am honored that you would think of me for this position. I truly am. But I can't say yes without thinking it over first, and I certainly can't answer for John. Could you give me some time to pray about this and discuss it with my brother? I promise, I won't keep you waiting too long."

"I understand, Chuck. Please take some time to pray about this. I'm confident once you do, God will make his plan clear to you."

"I'll have an answer for you soon, I'm sure. Have a good night, Joshua."

*****

John sat staring at the fire, not saying a word. Chuck had just finished outlining Joshua's proposal and was waiting for his brother's opinion.

As John turned to face his brother, the color creeping up his face spoke volumes. "Chuck, this mission nonsense has gone on long enough. Serving there was never part of our plan. You roped me into this quest of yours, and now that something is really starting to happen, you're abandoning me. What was all this for? It seems to me like you've made up your mind what you want to do. It's very kind of Joshua to want to include me on his board of directors, I've been happy to donate to his mission, but I'm a farmer, and a farmer has responsibilities. With running the farms down here, there's simply not enough hours in the day to chase off down a bunch of other rabbit trails. Somebody has to stay home and manage our land—especially if my brother and partner is going to abandon me and leave me to run everything myself! Chuck, we're the landowners now! If we never wanted to plow another field, we wouldn't have to! How can you just throw all of that away?"

"Brother, I'm not throwing anything away, and please don't think I'm abandoning you. That's not my intent at all. As I recall, the quest was about finding a way to get more. At first, I thought 'more' meant just more money, but I've come to realize there are many different kinds of 'more' that have nothing to do with finances. Having more also means having the option to branch out into other ventures. And I've also learned that having more brings with it a responsibility to share with others, just like Mr. Sellers and Mr. Johnson and Mr. Hillman and all the other men we've come to know have done with us.

"John, we could both move to Oklahoma City. You and I both know we could find a responsible man to run the farming operation down here. We'd still have the income from the land and the income from our oil. Also, David says I have a natural nose for sniffing out good investments. Don't you see, John? We don't need to put all our eggs in the same basket. We're not just limited to being farmers. We can be men who engage in many different kinds of business and who also make a positive difference in the lives of others through our involvement with the mission. Won't you join me?"

"Chuck, we finally have hope that we can live a better life than what we were living and what our ancestors lived before us. God has blessed us, just as we asked him to, and now you're just gonna throw it all back in his face."

"Let's talk about hope for a minute, John. You've been to the mission. You've seen the men who come through there. You, yourself, commented that there are men standing in the soup line every day wearing fine coats—coats that cost more than we once made in a year. Yet there they are, waiting in line for charity. They sleep on the cots in the mission because they have no home to return to each night. They've lost just about everything. These men probably never thought they'd be where they are today. They put their hope in money, and that money failed them. I'm not saying there's anything wrong with money, I'm just saying, after what I've seen, putting your hope in money is an awful lot like building your house on sand. One shift of the ground and we're in the soup line."

"I don't feel like we're putting all of our trust in just one thing. We've got the crops from the farms and the oil from the land to count on. Our eggs aren't all in one basket," said John.

"I see what you're saying, John, but I have to disagree. Whether it's crops or oil, it's all about money. What I want is what I've seen in the eyes of some of the men standing in line. I've looked into their eyes and seen a hope so secure, seems like nothing could shake it. These men have no job, no money, some have lost their families, and yet they are able to encourage me. Why? Because they've found the one thing they can trust in that will never fail them. The one thing that does not change like shifting shadows. They've found a real relationship with God. They've put all their trust in him and determined to follow him, no matter where he might lead them. That's what my friend Bill at the mission is doing. That's what Joshua is doing. And that, brother, is what I intend to do. I'm going to follow hard after God, wherever he takes me. If that means I hang on to my bank account and use the money that comes in there to help others find God, then so be it. If that means I give up a comfortable life to follow him, I'm still in. Ultimately, God is the only sure thing, so that's where I'm putting all my trust."

"So what about our farms? What about the oil royalties? What are you going to do? I can tell you right now, I'm staying put, with or without you."

"If you don't intend to join me in the city, I will sign over my share of the farms to you. It doesn't seem fair that I would reap any financial benefit when I'm not here to work alongside you. I'm sure

Mr. Johnson can help me get the paperwork together. I intend to keep my mineral rights to all the land and will continue to receive oil royalties, but the land itself will belong to you alone. Unless you'll reconsider. Brother, I'm absolutely convinced God has blessed us so we can bless others. Won't you join me in this new quest?"

John looked at the floor for a while before looking up at his brother. When their eyes met, John's were filled with tears. "I can't. I love you more than anyone in this world, but I can't leave behind what I've worked so hard to build. I'm sorry, Chuck."

*****

"So you see my predicament, sir." Chuck had just finished explaining Joshua's offer to Mr. Johnson.

"I do see what you're saying. And your brother has refused to join you in the city?"

"Yes, sir. He says his place is on the farm. I just don't understand why he can't see that we can do so much more if we'll just step out and trust God to lead us."

"That's a wise perspective, Chuck. You've been on a quest to improve your station in life and God has certainly been faithful. He's sent people into your path who have shared wisdom with you. God has also blessed you abundantly with material possessions—and all in a very short timeframe. So many people would have seen these material blessings as evidence of God's hand in their lives and so they would have continued to pursue hard after more of that blessing. It could only be the wisdom of God that has kept you from falling into that trap.

"Jesus said, 'What does it profit a man to gain the whole world but lose his soul?' When you've had 'the whole world,' you learn that it doesn't satisfy. Only when you follow the plan of the One who made you can you find true satisfaction.

"I'll get started preparing the paperwork to sign over your portion of the land to your brother. I know this decision has not been easy for you, but I want you to consider an old quote from a minister who lived in the 1600s that goes like this: 'He is no fool who parts with that which he cannot keep, when he is sure to be recompensed with that which he cannot lose.' If you start to doubt your decision, think in terms of eternity. There's a peace that comes when you pursue something that will never fade away. Perhaps you're being given the opportunity to do that now. Just remember, when you've found what you're looking for, you have an obligation to pass it along to the next person. I've come to believe that the secret to real change in this world is for everyone to faithfully impact those in their sphere of influence for God. Then as God increases your sphere, you have a responsibility to increase your vision to bring about change."

EPILOGUE

Chuck picked up his rag and wiped another table. It seemed the lines were getting longer every day. The news was not good. Crop prices had been in decline for a few years and now the drought was wiping out folks entirely. It was looking like not even oil could save Oklahoma now. The market had been glutted with the oil discoveries in east Texas and prices had dropped. Chuck had never seen such grim news hitting on every front.

But looking across the dining room, a smile spread across his face. There was his wife, Reba, chatting with a mother and child who had come to the mission for help. Reba had been volunteering at the mission since before Chuck got involved. When they married and she moved to the city, she started volunteering full-time and intended to continue doing so until they started having children.

Bill, one of the first men Chuck met when he came to visit the mission, was serving the last of the friends in the soup line. Bill's life was a testament to the redeeming power of God. Bill was no longer a patron of the mission; he was its director. Chuck had increased his giving to the mission significantly and had managed to persuade a few of his investor friends to do the same. Using these gifts, Joshua was able to open an additional mission up the road in Tulsa to help the growing number needy souls there.

Chuck was visiting with a friend at a table near the back, when Reba put her hand on his shoulder. "I'm so sorry to interrupt, but I need you for just a moment, Chuck."

Chuck excused himself and stepped aside with Reba. He could tell immediately by the look on her face that something was troubling her. "Chuck, I don't know how to say this, so I'm going to come right out with it. John just walked in to the mission."

"John, my brother? Excellent! Where is he? It's been too long since I last saw him!"

"Chuck, you don't understand. He walked into the mission as a patron. He's over in the soup line right now."

Chuck looked across the room and saw his brother. He couldn't believe how much John had aged. How long had it been since they'd seen each other face-to-face? Two years? Three? He couldn't remember. Once he moved to Oklahoma City, he'd been so busy serving on the board at the mission and expanding his stock holdings, he hadn't had time to get back to the farm. He'd kept up with some of the news from back home and knew farmers everywhere were falling on hard times, but he'd assumed John was fine.

He waited for John to be served and seated and then made his way over to the table. "Brother, it's so good to see you," Chuck said.

John stood and embraced his brother, then both men took seats at the table. "I guess you're wondering why I'm here, huh? Chuck, I've made a terrible mess of things."

"What's happened? I know the drought has to have taken a toll on your crops, but is there more?"

"Oh, Chuck, I've made such a mess. I'm afraid I've gone and lost everything. I don't know what happened. I faithfully put aside twenty percent of my income, ever since that first cotton crop you and I brought in. I continued to expand my land holdings, and one day, a certain parcel of land I'd had my eye on for years came available. Problem was, I didn't have enough cash on hand to make the purchase, so I leveraged that year's crops. I figured that I'd be able to pay back the note just as soon as I brought in the first harvest from that new land. Then the skies shut up like steel. Not only did my new land not yield like I thought it would, my other land produced only paltry harvests, and when I took what I had to market, the prices I received wouldn't pay the note.

"I started dipping into my savings. After all, isn't that what we'd put it back for? Another bad growing season brought on another dip into the savings. Didn't take long until my savings was gone. So I

112

sold my share of the mineral rights. I just knew the drought couldn't go on forever, and once it started raining again, I'd have my land and would be able to replace all that money I'd lost. But the drought has gone on long enough to wipe me completely out. Chuck, I coasted into town on what little gas I have left in my car. I'm going to try to sell the car and am hoping that you'll let me stay here at the mission until the car sells and I can find a job and a place to live."

"John, you're my brother. You will stay with me at my house and I will find you a job. You're a good man and a hard worker."

"Chuck, I'm not looking for you to clean up the mess I've made. I know it's my fault I'm in this predicament. I just need a little help until I can get back on my feet."

"I have no doubt God led me here to the city. He has blessed me with a nose to sniff out good values in the stock market. I call it horse sense, but really, I know this is a gift God has put inside me. These days, when other people are losing their shirts, I've managed to continue to grow my accounts. I know you have some of that same horse sense in you. I want to work alongside you again. I need to work alongside my brother.

"John, since the day I was born, you have been my constant companion. You've been my brother and my best friend. Anytime I needed help, I knew my big brother would be there for me. What kind of man would I be if I turned my back on you now?"

Tears were streaming down John's face. He didn't know how to respond to his brother's unconditional love. "I should have listened to you all those years ago. I was so horrible to you. I accused you of abandoning me. The truth is, I abandoned you and made you continue on your quest alone. I can't believe after all I've done, that you're willing to extend me such kindness."

"Today in my quiet time with God, I read the story from Matthew 19:16–30. Do you remember that story?"

Someone came to Jesus with this question: "Teacher, what good deed must I do to have eternal life?"

"Why ask me about what is good?" Jesus replied. "There is only One who is good. But to

answer your question—if you want to receive eternal life, keep the commandments."

"Which ones?" the man asked.

And Jesus replied: "'You must not murder. You must not commit adultery. You must not steal. You must not testify falsely. Honor your father and mother. Love your neighbor as yourself.'"

"I've obeyed all these commandments," the young man replied. "What else must I do?"

Jesus told him, "If you want to be perfect, go and sell all your possessions and give the money to the poor, and you will have treasure in heaven. Then come, follow me." But when the young man heard this, he went away sad, for he had many possessions.

"What I've found, as I've traveled on my journey, is that every time I've been willing to give up certain things for God, He has always paid me back at least a hundredfold. I gave up my title to our land—God blessed me with the ability to make wise investments. I gave up a life of living and working alongside my brother—now, God has brought us back together. It's so hard to open up your hands the first time God calls you to let something go, but the more times you do it, the more you realize that God's wisdom is always greater than our wisdom. If only we can get out of the way, He will accomplish his plans in our lives.

"With each new day that dawns, we have to ask ourselves if we will follow God on the never-ending quest to know his heart for us. Today, I'm thankful my brother has answered yes to that question and has rejoined me on the quest. Like the wise man once said, good company in a journey makes the way seem shorter, and with God's help, we will surely arrive safely at our final destination."

ABOUT THE AUTHOR

Dan Newberry is an author, speaker, entrepreneur, businessman, and former Oklahoma State Senator. Newberry has been a business professional in the mortgage banking industry for over eighteen years and currently serves as the Sr. Vice President of Lending for a federal credit union. Newberry was elected to the Oklahoma State Senate in 2008 and served as Majority Whip and Chairman of the Business and Commerce Committee. Newberry has received numerous awards for his work in economic policy, including the Guardian of Free Enterprise and the National Federation of Independent Businesses Guardian of Small Business awards. In 2012, Newberry became a distinguished Henry Toll Fellow. After attending a funeral at Arlington Cemetery for a fallen Oklahoma Soldier, Newberry created the Gold Star Medal of Honor to be given to the families of Oklahoma Soldiers killed in action. Newberry and his wife, Laura, founded the Paul Revere Reading Society, and assist challenged children overcome illiteracy through therapy dogs. The Newberry's reside in Tulsa, Oklahoma, with their four children and bull-mastiff, Ike.

CPSIA information can be obtained
at www.ICGtesting.com
Printed in the USA
FFHW022208250119
50288121-55329FF